Dear Romance Reader,

Welcome to a world of breathtaking passion and never-ending romance.
Welcome to *Precious Gem Romances*.

It is our pleasure to present *Precious Gem Romances*, a wonderful new line of romance books by some of America's best-loved authors. Let these thrilling historical and contemporary romances sweep you away to far-off times and places in stories that will dazzle your senses and melt your heart.

Sparkling with joy, laughter, and love, each *Precious Gem Romance* glows with all the passion and excitement you expect from the very best in romance. Offered at a great affordable price, these books are an irresistible value—and an essential addition to your romance collection. Tender love stories you will want to read again and again, *Precious Gem Romances* are books you will treasure forever.

Look for fabulous new *Precious Gem Romances* each month—available only at Wal★Mart.

Kate Duffy
Editorial Director

D1570638

SWEET ENEMY

Shelley Bradley

Zebra Books
Kensington Publishing Corp.
http://www.zebrabooks.com

ZEBRA BOOKS are published by

Kensington Publishing Corp.
850 Third Avenue
New York, NY 10022

First Printing: April, 1999
10 9 8 7 6 5 4 3 2 1

Printed in the United States of America

This book is dedicated to Four Extraordinary
Women—My Grandmothers:

Liz Blee
Ruth Plunkett
Marion Reid
Danna Robson

You've all given me the best parts of you to carry in
my heart. I'm richer for having loved you.

Prologue

London
January, 1750

Heavy iron cuffs chafed the red, raw skin of his wrists, mimicking the festering in his soul. His arms, suspended from chains affixed to the ceiling, had ceased hurting hours ago. Now, they hung useless and numb—unlike his rage, his hate.

Dominic Grayson shivered from the winter chill and closed his eyes against the dim, dirty cell, pretending he was home. But his mind's eye shattered the illusion, flashing a vision of his wife's bruised, twisted corpse that had ended his hopes for the future and banished him here, Newgate Prison.

Leaning his bruised cheek against the wet, frozen wall, he struggled to escape the ever-present sound of the other prisoners' moans in the cramped cells beside his. He focused on Phillip Dowling. Anger and retribution, his constant cell mates, flooded Dominic.

A moment later, a key grated in the lock of his cell door. He tensed, hostility raging through him. Or was it fear? Through swollen eyes, he surveyed the incoming guard.

"Enjoyin' yerself, Grayson?" the jailer sneered.

"Go to hell, Boyd," Dominic growled, surging against his bonds. Paralyzing needles of pain erupted in each fingertip. Rivulets of fresh blood trickled down his arms. He cursed. Come morning, the guards would indulge in dousing the wounds with salt water, then enjoy his sweat and pain.

Boyd cackled. "Give up, killer. Ye ain't goin' to escape."

Give up on freedom, surrender his life? He gritted his teeth. "I *will* escape."

"You'll die tryin', more like. Or the buggers at Old Bailey will see to yer execution. Mark me words."

A jolt of raw fury thundered through him. He kicked out, his feet nearly connecting with Boyd's stomach. Cursing a retort, the guard swung, his fist striking the underside of Dominic's chin. The prisoner's head snapped back, striking the craggy wall behind him. Biting back a moan, Dominic swore not to give the guard the pleasure of witnessing his pain.

"That'll teach ye humility, ye bloody knave. If not, Eddie'll carry on in the mornin'."

"No doubt." Dominic's voice flared with contempt before he spat in Boyd's greasy face.

The guard wiped the spittle away with his sleeve, then backhanded Dominic's bruised cheek. "For that, I'll leave yer food where ye can smell it and watch the rats nibble on it. Maybe hunger'll teach you a lesson, ye bastard."

The black-clad man set the tray at his feet. Dominic inched closer, enticed by the sole source of heat in the underground cell. He barely noticed the guard make his way across the filthy floor and slam the wooden door behind him.

Dominic inhaled the steaming scent of the gruel, his

insides clawing with hunger. Two days ago he had forced himself to eat the grisly slop he had been served. That meal had been his last. This gut-wrenching starvation tortured his mind as much as his body. His stomach coiled in pain. God, would he ever leave prison alive?

Resisting the dismal thought, he vowed again to escape his dank, four-by-four cell—and the dismal darkness enveloping his soul. *Revenge,* he forced himself to think; *you will have it and be free.* But he knew escape would be next to impossible when he remained chained at the wrists and ankles.

How ironic, he thought, that he'd been forced to squander seven months of his life in Newgate. As he recalled, the prison's front arch bore four figures representing Liberty, Peace, Security, and Plenty. He'd been treated to none of those in this hell. With a bitter grunt, he wondered again if he would ever receive a trial—or simply be executed.

Daily, the magistrate's officials grilled him with questions. No one believed he was innocent of the heinous murder, for he had no alibi—and every reason to have wished her dead. He was denied contact with any legal counsel. Every damned night, he listened to hungry rats scurrying about his bare feet. If he slept at all, he woke to the hideous smells of mildew, urine, and excrement to face another day of pain and uncertainty.

Revenge supplied him a reason to survive. Dominic spent hours each day devising painful tortures for Phillip Dowling—his one-time friend, the man responsible for his wife Marcella's brutal murder. The fiend who had framed him for the crime. Phillip would pay with everything sacred to him, Dominic vowed.

The shuffle of footsteps outside the cell interrupted his thoughts. The key scraped within its lock.

"Who's there?" Dominic asked, masking his cold fear. Nighttime executions were always a possibility.

"Keep your voice down," a tall, unfamiliar man hissed. "I've come to help you escape."

Dominic peered suspiciously, noting the man wore the black garb of a prison guard. "Why should I believe you?"

The intruder cast a nervous glance down the hall, then stepped inside. "Because I've risked my life."

A painful surge of hope burst inside Dominic, yet caution dashed it with logic. The man's height and stature were similar to his own. But the stranger had the advantage; he was not chained like a dangerous animal.

"You could shoot me after you 'free' me, and no one would give a damn. How do I know Phillip hasn't sent you to do what the Crown has neglected to do thus far?"

"I knocked two guards unconscious and stole one's clothing." He produced a ring of keys from his breeches. "Would I do that to shoot you?"

"You might, if Phillip Dowling paid you enough."

The bearded man reached for a wrist shackle and tried one key after another, flinching when they rattled. "If the duke of Dalmont had paid me to kill you, I could slit your throat now and no one would care. Damn you, we haven't much time. Trust me!"

"And if I don't?" Suspicion shadowed Dominic's voice.

"What are your choices?" he whispered. "To stay here, in this hell?"

Dominic said nothing, knowing the stranger was right.

At last, one key fit, and the man uttered a soft sound

of triumph. As silently as possible, he unshackled Dominic's wrists. "Now, be quiet."

Dominic lowered his stiff appendages slowly, gnashing his teeth as blood rushed in, bringing acute pain.

The stranger freed Dominic's legs. "If you can walk, we have a better chance of escape."

"I can."

The first few steps were excruciating. After months of almost total inactivity, the muscles in his leaden legs protested his commands. Clenching his fists against the pain, he plodded out of his cell after the other man.

In the corridor, they maneuvered around an unconscious, nearly naked guard. With grim satisfaction, Dominic recognized Boyd, the one who had brought his meal minutes ago. Again, a dangerous hope surfaced within him.

Cautiously, he followed the man from the condemned felon's hold in the basement up the stairs, then round a corner. Dominic glimpsed the prison's back exit ahead. Elation surged through him; freedom loomed moments from his grasp.

Suddenly, a sentry emerged from a black corridor and darted in their path. Dominic tensed, praying his rescuer could bribe or fool the guard. If not, recapture meant instant death.

Dominic pictured his wife's corpse and Phillip's gloating face upon his arrest. Fear surged power through Dominic. He leaped forward, smashing his fist into the guard's jaw. An audible smack followed as he hit his target, sending the uniformed man careening into the wall.

The guard shook his head, as if to clear it, then opened his mouth to shout. The stranger rammed his knee into the guard's groin. Crumpling to the ground like a wounded animal, the sentry moaned and clutched his genitals. Dominic's rescuer kicked the guard in the head. The uniformed man fell back, unconscious.

The man helped Dominic over the guard's prone form. Moments later, they bolted through the door, past two guards sleeping off the effects of too much gin, and emerged into the crisp night.

Freedom! Dominic paused, reveling as elation rushed to greet him in the winter wind stirring across his face. Finally, he was free, and he vowed nothing, no one, would *ever* change that again.

The man whirled away and led Dominic to a pair of horses hidden at the back of a hill, winter-dry and windswept.

The stranger handed him the reins. "Ride as far from here as you can tonight. Do not stop. The morning guards will notice your absence soon. They'll sound an alarm and begin the search."

"Who are you?" Dominic asked, torn between suspicion and gratitude.

The stranger extended his hand. Hesitantly, Dominic shook it. "Andrew Seaton."

The name meant nothing to Dominic. "Why did you risk your life to help me?"

Andrew shoved him toward a horse. "We have no time to talk now. In a week, I'll meet you in Cambridge under the Bridge of Sighs. We'll find a safe place to hide you then."

Dominic hesitated, still only half-trusting this stranger with vague motives. But what choice did he have? He nodded before he turned and mounted.

Dominic rode away unchallenged, and the realization

he was free pumped through him. Now he had hope, not only because he'd been rescued, but also because he could make his fantasy of revenge against Phillip Dowling a reality.

One

London
March, 1751

Butterflies dancing in her stomach, Victoria placed her gloved hand in her father's outstretched one and stepped from the black-lacquered coach. With a palm above her brow, she shielded her eyes from the afternoon sun. The cool spring wind struck her face, blowing corkscrew tendrils of auburn hair from its stiff-frilled cap.

The towering St. James town house before her glowed an incandescent white in the dying sunlight. She scanned the red geraniums and bricked walkway slowly, her excitement mounting.

Tomorrow she would be wed.

Victoria gazed at her father. His blue eyes glowed.

"You'll make a fine bride, love."

"Because you and Mama have taught me what love should be."

With a fatherly smile, he patted her hand and guided her toward her betrothed, the duke of Dalmont.

Victoria knew she was lucky that her parents wanted her to marry for love. And though she had only met the duke of Dalmont thrice, she saw no reason they could not fall in love. He was, at least until tomorrow, one of the *ton's* wealthiest bachelors. He appreciated art, which was her passion. And he was handsome.

As if her thoughts had conjured Dalmont up, he opened the door. Victoria studied his green brocade-clad, bewigged figure, holding in a sigh. On black, square-toed shoes, he sauntered towards them.

"Hello, Montgomery," the blond-haired man called. "A pleasure to see you again."

Her father smiled widely, as did Victoria, excitement bubbling within her.

"The pleasure is mine," her father assured the man.

"Yes. And Lady Victoria." Dalmont took her hand, bringing it a breath short of his lips. "You look beautiful beyond words. I shall have to consult a famous poet to justly describe you." His pale eyes flashed with appreciation.

Victoria grinned at him. She supposed she looked foolish at best, lovesick at worst. But a girl could get used to such compliments for life.

"Since I don't happen to know any famous poets, I shall leave that to you," she teased.

"It will be my pleasure to hound one until he writes an appropriate stanza on your behalf."

Casting her gaze to the floor to hide her blush, she smiled again. Yes, she could get used to hearing this each day.

Victoria's gaze found its way back to Dalmont. A gold-trimmed emerald coat draped elegantly about his knees. Crisp ivory lace adorned his wrists. Perfectly polished shoes gleamed in the room's light, making him look the picture of aristocratic perfection.

He stood six inches taller than her own five feet, four inches. Best of all, he epitomized the dashing fantasy husband she had conjured up in her young dreams—handsome, gallant, witty. Tomorrow they would begin their life, soon sharing affection, contentment, and love.

Nothing could mar her happiness now.

Dominic Grayson crept into Dalmont's town house, fury swirling through him like a windstorm.

The town house's kitchen had changed little since his days of friendship with the killer—same wooden counters, same inviting smell of warm bread.

Yet so much had changed.

Now he was here for a purpose, one that would alter his life—and Dalmont's. One that could give him the tools to cast aside his anger. But he feared he would never live freely again, without fear of capture and execution.

He crept across the deserted kitchen, then settled into a black corner to wait. Within seconds, Corinne trod into the room, humming a soft tune. Candlelight shone in golden tones across half her youthful face as she put an empty tray away.

Dominic grabbed her arm, then pulled her against his chest. Immediately, she gasped.

Dominic covered her mouth with his hand. "Shh. It's only me."

Corinne turned to him, whispering, "Nicky, ye came back!"

With a smile, he looked down into her flushed oval face. "Of course I did. I had no intention of neglecting you, despite the fact coming here is dangerous. Though I doubt you've been lacking in male companionship."

She giggled quietly and sent a saucy expression his way. "No, but I 'ave missed ye. Now that ye've come," she began, pretending to adjust a button on his shirt, "I deserve yer attention."

The corner of Dominic's mouth twisted upward. "Later," he replied. "Now, we must talk. I have a plan and need your help."

She leaned against him, her lips touching a sensitive spot behind his ear. "Ye know I'll do whatever ye ask, Nicky."

"Tell me of this girl Phillip plans to wed tomorrow."

Corinne paused before saying, "She's lovely, no mistakin' that. And she seems well pleased with the match."

Dominic grunted in frustration. "So the wench has no more sense than a back-alley mutt. Damn!" He raked a hand through his hair. "And what of Phillip? Is the high and mighty duke of Dalmont still smitten?"

"Aye, 'tis clear he is," Corinne said. "What do ye plan?"

Dominic paced away, moving to the window. Lifting the drape a fraction, he peered outside. Phillip's guard at the entrance to Pall Mall still slept soundly. And no wonder, as he was clearly fond of gin. "Let's just say Phillip will wake to quite a shock tomorrow morn."

Corinne bit her bottom lip. "Nicky, I'm not likin' the sound of that. Whatever ye plan is dangerous."

"Have faith in me, will you? If I stop Phillip's marriage to this girl, I can avenge my loss."

The maid turned her face away. "Nothing will bring Lady Marcella back. She's gone to the Lord, Nicky."

"A fact I feel every single day," he said bitterly.

"Ye should not to do this."

"Why? I will die anyway if I am caught. And as long as I am free, I can avenge Marcella's seduction and murder."

"How?" she breathed, as if afraid of the answer.

Dominic's mouth turned up into a cold smile. "Corinne, pack a satchel of Lady Victoria's belongings.

Tonight, set it just inside her room. Make sure she has enough laudanum to make her . . . comfortable for a spell."

"You're taking her, are ye?"

"You ask too many questions."

Corinne's mouth turned down in a pout. "Will ye bed her?"

He avoided her question with an arched brow. "Is that a note of jealousy I hear?"

Corinne cocked her dark head coquettishly. "Even if ye bed 'er, it will mean nothing to ye but revenge, ain't that so?"

With a devilish grin, he pushed away from the wall and crossed the narrow room. When he reached her, his broad palms cradled her hips. "Exactly."

With a nod, Corinne raised a hand to his hair and drew his mouth to hers. In response, Dominic's palms caressed the coarse fabric down the length of her back, then lower.

"Can ye stay?" she asked, breathless and throaty.

He shook his head. "I have too much to do."

She nodded, not at all happily. "Watch yourself, Nicky."

"You be careful around Phillip. He'll hurt you for helping me if he suspects anything."

She smiled. "Never fear. I can watch me own back."

Dominic nodded, then added, "Don't forget the instructions I gave you. You must follow them precisely."

"Count on me, Nicky. As long as ye need me, I'll be here."

Victoria sipped the sherry Corinne had unexpectedly brought. Grimacing at its unusually sweet taste, she set the half-full glass aside. She rose and wandered through the garden, conscious of the beauty of the spring foliage visible in the torch-lit dimness. Gladioli stalks of various colors stood proudly, boasting delicate pastel petals. She plucked a climbing rose of the purest white. Then spotting a ladybug, she coaxed it onto her finger.

She gazed at the red-winged bug, feeling as if she'd flown away to a magical place where dreams came true. Dalmont was all she'd ever wanted in a husband, handsome and kind. True, she did not know him well. But her parents, whose loving kind of marriage she wanted for herself, said Dalmont was a good man.

She sighed, for tomorrow all her dreams would come true.

The unexpected tap of footsteps interrupted her reverie.

Turning to the sound, she watched a man in dark clothing slink through the garden. He was heavily armed, from the firearm slung over his shoulder to the wicked knife sheathed to his thigh. She caught a glimpse of his bearded, scarred face before he disappeared from the light.

A chill skipped up her spine. Her eyes and her senses told her he was dangerous. A tinge of cold fear made its way up her chest. Why was the man here?

Without further thought, Victoria followed him. Somehow, she would stop him from his nefarious purpose, find a footman or servant to help her. She had the advantage of surprise.

Just before she careened around a corner, a man's voice stopped her short. "Where the bloody hell have you been?"

The impatient whisper rang in her head. Dalmont? Instinctively, she slipped behind a wall of creeping ivy and listened to the muffled rumble of another man's voice, answering.

"Never mind," Phillip hissed. "Did you find him?"

"No, he is not on the town house's grounds."

"He must be. I can feel it. He knows I'm to wed Lady Victoria tomorrow. Now would be the perfect opportunity for Dominic Grayson to wreak his vengeance."

Who was this Dominic Grayson that he worried Dalmont so? Try as she might, Victoria did not remember her betrothed ever mentioning the man. And for what would the man seek revenge?

"Your Grace, he has not been seen in a month. Maybe he fled the country."

Victoria heard Phillip's boot heels pace across the tile. "He is close, I promise you. I know the cunning bastard better than to think he has given up. He cannot abide people believing he killed that whore."

Though she heard him as if he spoke from far away, Victoria recoiled against the venom in Dalmont's voice. Why would Dalmont have anything to do with something less than a lady? Shaking her head to clear the descending fog, she listened on.

"What shall I do if I see him?" asked the stranger.

"Grayson has made my life hell since his escape from Newgate. I want him dead."

A chill swept through Victoria despite her weariness. Her husband-to-be, the man who would make her dream marriage a reality, had ordered the murder of another man—and so calmly! Sweet Mary! Pressing her palm over weighty eyes, she wondered what she truly knew of her intended.

The stranger asked, "And the other matter?"

"Yes, Lady Victoria. I want her. If Dominic knows that, he will act, possibly against her. He may even kill her."

Victoria stifled a gasp behind her hand. Kill her? Dominic Grayson was a stranger to her. Why would he?

"What shall I do?" asked the other man.

"Keep searching for Grayson. I will see to my bride."

Again, the man grunted, then swung away.

Incredulity and a conflicting warmth flowed through Victoria, mixing with a liquid drowsiness she couldn't shake. She stood with her hands pressed to the stone wall for balance until Phillip's footsteps clicked away. A cry trapped within her, she stumbled to the French doors and back into the solarium. Tiredly, she bolted the door with trembling fingers. The cold metal against her fingers pierced her consciousness.

Leaning against the door for support, she drew several calming breaths before journeying on to her chamber. *Think, think,* she admonished herself.

A haze had descended over her mind. Who was this Dominic Grayson? A blackguard who had done something terrible to her betrothed, who might end her life? She struggled to solve the riddle. No answers materialized. Only one thought occupied her tired mind: was there indeed a vengeful madman prowling around Dalmont's town house intent on having her blood?

Two

Victoria tried to raise her head from the pillow min-utes—or perhaps hours—later, feeling a cold stare upon her in the near darkness. Fear brought her more fully awake.

It was impossible that anyone watched her, logic re-minded. How could anyone have stolen into her room? Corinne had securely locked every entrance.

Perhaps there was an entrance she knew nothing about. Had somebody crept into the room before her? Such made no sense.

Her sleep-heavy gaze shifted around the room, but the surrounding darkness seemed impossible to pierce. The feeling of hot eyes upon her grew more intense with each moment. Her heart pounded in a furious rhythm, replacing lethargy with consciousness. Imagi-nation warred with common sense in the heavy silence.

"I can feel your presence," she said.

She could, stronger than before. An insidious coil of fear twisted itself around her, tangling with her urge to flee.

"Show yourself!" she demanded, hoping the feeling was no more than fancy.

Lightning flashed, brightening the shadowy room in a startling flare of brilliance. In that moment, she glimpsed a menacing figure looming above her, his flat-brimmed hat pulled low.

Dark descended again.

Gasping in terror, Victoria inched away from the face-less menace, across her bed, her back to the wall. She opened her mouth to scream, but heart-pounding fear and mind-numbing shock smothered the sound.

A frightening shadow, clothed completely in black, hovered over her, seething a hostility that made her skin break out in a cold sweat.

A rattling clap of thunder clanged a moment later, rumbling its power in Victoria's ears, intensifying her fright.

Through the shadows, she watched the intruder take a step toward her. She bolted out of bed and dashed to the door. Thoughts chased one another through her head in an illogical circle, mounting her chaos. Who was this dastard? Why did he stand in her chamber, his face the epitome of hatred?

She strained over her shoulder, searching for the evil figure, but her gaze could no longer pierce the near blackness. Yet, she sensed he was close, felt him breathing behind her. She ran faster. Fatigue invaded her muscles, making movement a monumental task.

Without warning, his large palm clamped over her mouth. An unyielding arm wrapped around her waist, cutting off her breath. He lifted her from the floor and dragged her against the wall. She felt his harsh, hot breath upon her cheek.

Terror and rage engulfing her, she clawed and struggled. He grabbed her arms and pinned them to her sides.

"Stop your struggles," he hissed.

Panting with fear and exertion, Victoria demanded, "What do you want from me?"

He gave no reply. He merely covered her mouth with a cloth. Victoria loosed a muffled scream. The man knotted the cloth at the back of her head, then turned her toward him again, as if she'd said nothing.

Lifting her like a sack of flour, he slung her over his shoulder. Her stomach met the bone and hard muscle beneath; the air left her lungs in a rush. Unable to breathe, Victoria felt powerless to struggle as the stranger crept out the door, down the servants' stairs, and out into the rain-tinged night.

Cold droplets hit her back as she struggled for each breath. Determined to escape, she braced her forearms against his back—and kicked. Her feet struck his abdomen with a satisfying thud. He grunted; his legs buckled beneath him. Together, they plummeted to the garden's muddy ground. Victoria straddled his chest, her face in the soil above his shoulder.

A sharp object cut into her forehead. She reached up to retrieve it, discovering a small, mud-covered rock. Her warm blood mingled with the wet soil and the rain on her face. She bit back a groan as she scrambled to her feet.

Her captor clasped her thighs, pulling her down. In one swift motion, he rolled her to her back, his position now the dominant one. He twisted his fingers through her wet hair and pulled her gaze to his. The chiseled planes of his hard, unfamiliar face, framed by hair as black as night, loomed dangerously close.

"Give up." Her captor clamped his fingers about her chin, holding her roughly. "You will not escape me."

The man rose, grasping her wrist, and hauled her toward a pair of horses waiting in the distance, just off

Pall Mall. He turned to one horse to check the ties holding a satchel, *her* satchel. She wondered how he'd obtained her belongings.

Mounting the black animal, he pulled her up in front of him so she, too, straddled the saddle. He hugged her tightly to his chest, preventing any further opportunity to escape.

The stranger paused, gazing at the town house, before he urged his mount forward and they shot down the road.

They traveled outside London's limits, through the mud and the deluge of rain. Her captor quickly charted their course from the main road. Certain the rain would destroy their tracks, she dreaded that no one could find her on this obscure road. God help her. She was truly alone with a man who seemed to care little for mercy.

Victoria awoke, feeling hard ground beneath her, a trickling sound in her ears. Struggling to open her eyes, despite her throbbing head, she found herself near a river, a small fire giving off needed warmth.

Above her, storm clouds covered the moon and dark sky. Her captor stood mere feet away, staring up at the night sky. All she could discern of his face was a hard, chiseled profile.

He was an imposing man, tall and broad. The breadth of his shoulders and the size of his hands alone convinced her he could easily kill her with little effort.

She heard him utter a curse so foul she blushed. Then, to her horror, he turned to face her. In the muted light, she could see the icy sparkle of his eyes and the angled planes of his angry face.

"I see you've awakened," he said.

"Who are you? What do you want with me?" she asked, struggling to sit up

Without answering, he handed her a flask and a chunk of bread. "Eat."

She thrust the food back at him. "I've no wish for food, only answers."

He pushed the bread back into her lap. "Later. Eat now."

Clearly, the brute only played by his rules. Deciding to placate him, she broke off a section of the small loaf and took a bite. She sipped water while she ate the bread, returning the flask when she finished.

"Now," she demanded, "take me back to my betrothed."

His icy gaze sliced to her, making her shiver. "Why?"

She frowned, having no wish to explain her hopes and wishes for the future to this fiend. True, she had experienced a moment's doubt when she'd overheard Dalmont order Grayson's murder; but he'd surely been protecting himself, nothing more.

She lifted her chin. "Because he is to be my husband."

His expression was one of total unconcern. "He *was* to have been your husband. That is no longer possible."

Images of her ideal marriage and ideal husband gave her courage. "But you must free me. I—I love Dalmont."

At that, her captor's expression transformed to one of amusement.

"Really?" He paused, as if assessing the information. "You sound uncertain."

"I'm not!" she protested. "Dalmont is a wonderful man and I will come to love him."

He frowned, eyes narrowing. "You will come to love him? Did you not say you loved him now?"

Victoria paused, struggling for an answer to his veritable riddle. "I scarcely know him, but—"

"You scarcely know him. Do you always purport to love strangers?" he mocked. "If so, you could love me."

Victoria gave him a hard laugh. "You are not the kind of man a woman can love—thieving her from her bed, dragging her through the rain. If that is your idea of courting, you've much to learn."

His tense face darkened with fury. "I haven't come courting."

She turned a burning glare on him. "Then you'll return me to Dalmont?"

He grabbed her arms and demanded, "Why do you want to marry him, besides the feelings you believe will develop?"

She jerked her arm from his grasp. "Don't touch me!"

"You misunderstand who gives the orders." His eyes, his face, turned hard. "Tell me why you sought to wed Dalmont."

"My parents wished it," she snapped.

"That is the only reason?' Dominic questioned suspiciously.

She hesitated. "Yes."

"A very dutiful daughter," he mocked, releasing her.

Victoria scrambled to her feet, away from him. In horror, she watched the stranger stalk toward her again.

"Now, what is it you *really* seek?" he demanded.

He came closer still, anchoring his hands to the tree behind her, trapping her against the rough, barky trunk. As her mind raced, she ducked beneath his arm and sprinted away. The stranger caught her wrist and backed her against the tree once more.

Fear, rage, and his presence, all hot and looming,

smothered her. She wanted to cry or scream. She did neither.

"You haven't answered me. Why did you agree to this marriage?"

"My concerns are not yours," she answered through gritted teeth.

His hand latched onto her arm and gave a warning squeeze. "I suggest you tell me now."

Victoria hesitated, loath to tell the brute anything. Yet she realized that presenting a picture of docility might fool him into letting down his guard as no battle would.

"Happiness," she grated out. "I want love in my marriage."

"Love?" he shot back.

Victoria took several deep breaths, growing braver with each. "I want a fine home, a caring husband, and happy children."

He paused, seeming to weigh her answer. "You've chosen the worst man in all of England, my lady."

She raised her chin, refusing to let him foster doubts within her. "Dalmont will well suit me, I have no fear. He is gentle and good, but a criminal like you wouldn't understand that."

He paused; nothing in his expression betrayed he'd even heard her insult. "Hear me well, you will never wed Dalmont, smitten though you both may be. You deserve each other, a scoundrel and a fool."

"I am no fool, only a woman who knows her mind. And I will escape to wed Dalmont."

The man shook his dark head. "Dalmont owes me a huge debt, lady. Through you, I will have revenge."

Revenge. Revenge. The word repeated itself in her head until the horror sank in. The truth of his identity hit her in an instant. "Oh, sweet heaven! I know who you are . . . Dominic Grayson." She continued search-ing her hazy memory. "You killed someone . . . a woman!"

His face turned to granite in an instant. "Yes, I am Dominic Grayson."

She gasped. If the villain had killed before, he would surely think little of killing again.

"Now you want to prevent my marriage to Dalmont. Why?"

The abrupt line of his jaw tensed ominously. "My reasons are my own."

Three

Victoria frowned against a piercing headache as she lay with her eyes closed, haunted by the image of a black-clad savage seething in the rain. The vision meant nothing, she told herself. Nothing at all.

Then she heard boot heels click across a hardwood floor.

Disorientation became fear as Victoria bolted upright in bed, eyes flying open, and realized she wasn't at Dalmont's town house. Nor was she alone.

She searched the unfamiliar room. Her gaze skimmed over worn furniture and her satchel before finding the menacing savage from her nightmares at a blackened hearth. Unfortunately, he was no apparition, but a real and dangerous enemy.

He stood lean and tall, his powerful stature slicing her with a new blade of trepidation. The snug fit of buff-colored breeches and black boots to the knee accentuated long legs and displayed the muscles of his thighs when he shifted his weight. A crisp, white linen shirt strained across the breadth of his shoulders, making Victoria aware that if he planned on killing her, thwarting him would be a challenge.

Her captor turned to face her, as if sensing her gaze

upon him. Victoria's heart pumped furiously, slamming against her chest.

Their eyes met. His jet brows rose assessingly, his gaze roving over her. Victoria clutched the blanket to her chest.

"Where am I?" she demanded, lunging from the bed, caring little for her rumpled night rail.

Without an answer, he turned back to the hearth.

"How long do you intend to keep me prisoner?"

He propped his booted foot on the hearth, draping his arm across one knee. "That depends on you."

She peered at him with suspicion. "I have a say in this?"

"To be sure."

Victoria peered at Grayson, refusing to trust his demeanor, which was entirely too amiable. "What must I do?"

His gaze strayed from her face, roamed across her shoulders . . . and lower. That stare felt hot on Victoria's skin.

"What do you want?" She feared his answer.

Beneath an ominous scowl, his hazel eyes blazed with a riot of emotions. He stepped closer, too close. Victoria inched back. He grabbed her wrists, halting her escape.

Pulling on her arms, Grayson brought her toward him. His unnerving, unwavering gaze probed her face, her eyes, trying to master her without a word. Refusing to give in, she glared back.

Grayson's jaw clenched as he clasped her against him, her breasts to the wall of his chest. "I want your virginity."

Shock and horror smothered her. Surely she hadn't heard him correctly. "My what?"

"Your virtue, my lady. You'll stay with me until I bed you."

With those hard-edged words, his expression turned forbidding. His determined gaze, fierce stance, and three-day's growth of beard lent him the look of a pirate.

She began struggling, sinking her teeth into his wrist, her fingernails in his neck. She tried shielding herself from his curses and ruthless grip. Grabbing her shoulders, Grayson jerked her closer, then imprisoned her wrists behind her.

Breathing harder now, he said, "Stop it. You merely waste your energy and mine."

"I won't surrender! My virtue is *mine* to give when I wed Dalmont."

He cursed. "It will be easier if you don't fight me."

"Easier for you, perhaps."

"You'd prefer to give your maidenhood to a man capable of beating a woman to death?"

Victoria's chin dropped to her chest as the gruesome image filled her mind. "Dalmont would never do as you did."

Cold fury flashed across his face, filling its dark contours with hatred. Victoria watched the transformation in shock. "Fool! He killed a woman named Marcella. He had seduced her, then beat her when he tired of her charms."

Swallowing hard, Grayson released her, then turned to pace. "Phillip framed me, for which he will pay dearly," he finally answered. "I shall see to it."

Dominic Grayson was clearly a man befuddled by delusions. Dalmont surely would not beat a woman to death. Deciding not to argue with her deranged captor, she asked, "If I agreed to . . . agreed to your plan, would I be free to leave . . . after?"

Grayson paused. One second . . . two; still he said nothing.

She seized on his silence. "I wouldn't be free to leave, would I? What else do you want?"

"Two things. First, an acknowledgment of Dalmont's guilt. He wants you to wife; and if he chooses to discard you in the same manner as Marcella, I could not forgive myself."

Frowning, Victoria stared at her captor. He believed he was saving her from death by abducting her and forcing his way into her bed. Definitely the man was demented.

"I will never believe Dalmont capable of such evil."

"Then we shall be together a very long time, indeed."

Refusing to take his bait, she prompted, "And your second stipulation?"

"That you stay with me for six months, the same length of time Dalmont kept Marcella."

Six months! The man was a raving lunatic, beyond doubt. "I will not denounce him, nor stay for such a ridiculous length of time. And I most certainly will not allow you in my bed!"

He lifted a hand to her cheek and caressed her, his touch disturbingly gentle. "I can make it pleasant."

She slapped his hand away, refusing to acknowledge the tingle dancing in the pit of her stomach. "Pleasant? Nothing about you could be pleasant. Anything you want from me, you'll have to take by force."

Victoria watched a muscle in his jaw tighten. She knew she had angered him, and though it surely meant danger, she was glad.

"Are you certain I won't do just that?"

Fear and pride warred for her voice. Pride won out. "Oh, I have no doubt you would force an unwilling woman, but I shall know I did everything possible to save myself."

His full mouth compressed in a grim line. "You have no idea what rape is like, my lady. Even the word is ugly. Imagine a determined man trapping you beneath him until you're helpless, then lifting your skirts and tearing your chemise. His unfamiliar hands will probe your bare flesh before he'll force himself between your legs. Then, he will violate—"

"Stop it!" His vivid words cast a hideous mental picture. "You seem well versed on the subject. From experience, perhaps?"

Without warning, he grasped her chin. "Unspeakable cruelties occur daily in Newgate, rape among them. I saw many, heard their screams, their cries, their pleas. I never committed one. But for revenge, I will." He released her wrists, standing with an angry shrug. "Think about that."

She was in a nightmare beyond her worst imagining. Now she would lose her chance at happiness—and her virtue by force—if Dominic Grayson succeeded.

"You've no right to inflict such torture on anyone!"

"I'm giving you a simple choice: Come to me willingly . . . or suffer my consequence."

Outraged, Victoria cried, "I will not consider this devil's bargain, not while there's a breath left in my body!"

"Then it will be your loss. If you don't have an answer for me in three days, I will make the decision myself."

"That soon?" Tears came to her eyes, constricting her throat. "Why in God's name are you doing this?"

"I told you, Lady Victoria," he answered tersely. "Revenge."

"My virginity will not bring your . . ." Lover? Sister? Victoria knew not who the woman had been to her captor. "Violating me will not bring Marcella back."

"You speak true." Grayson paralyzed her with a tumultuous hazel stare. "But Dalmont will feel the agony of knowing that his woman has lain with another."

Judging from the furied anguish on his hard face, Victoria surmised that Marcella had been Dominic Grayson's lover, perhaps his mistress. Or even his wife. She frowned, clasping trembling fingers before her. "What then? Do you plan to kill me as well?"

"I've no stomach for murdering women, as Phillip does."

"Only for rape, then." She tossed her hands in the air. "That is pure logic."

He scowled at her, but said nothing.

Grayson was dangerous. She knew beyond a doubt he was capable of rape. He would carry out his threat if she defied him.

Surrender was not an option. She needed to escape, but how? There was no one else in sight. She had no clue where he'd imprisoned her, except south of London. But maybe, if she could learn something, she could use it to her advantage and gain freedom.

After a moment's pause, she asked, "Where are we?"

His gaze sliced to hers, cutting through to her ploy. "Don't think you will be leaving without me. We are completely isolated in a steep canyon. No traveler will happen by to rescue you. You will not dash your way to freedom. There is but one way out, and I've blocked it with a gate taller than you and topped it with wooden stakes."

"So, I am trapped until I hand you my virtue and my future?"

He leaned closer, his face mere inches from hers, and shrugged. "View it however you will."

"You're cruel!" Victoria looked away from his hot gaze, bolstered by rage.

"And you, Lady Victoria, are too vocal."

Hatred spewed throughout her. She longed to hit him again, or scratch his eyes out, anything that would cause him pain. "You vulgar knave, I would love to see atrocities forced on you. It might give you the set-down you deserve."

The hard line of his jaw tightened. His voice was pure venom. "I *lived* an atrocity for two years, and it did not set me down. I chose to fight. That is why you're here."

"To be your pawn, you scoundrel?" She tossed a hostile glare in his direction.

"I care little for your sentiments, only that you make the right decision."

"And I suppose 'the right decision' would be to allow myself to become your whore?"

He shook his head. "I merely suggested it would be less difficult on us both if you did not resist my plans. And as I said, I will try to make it enjoyable."

"I will never want you!" she vowed.

"Don't say never, my lady. Anything is possible." His hazel eyes probed her, suggesting heated embraces between men and women Victoria had oft considered. Disturbed, she bristled from his touch and looked away.

"Not with the loathing I feel for you," she shot back.

"That is your choice. I'm infinitely more interested in revenge than your sentiments for me."

Releasing her arm, he strode out the door.

* * *

Victoria sat in stunned silence. How could this be happening to her? She was God knew where, betrothed to an angel, captive of the devil himself. This bizarre nightmare was happening so quickly, and none of it made sense.

Who was Dominic Grayson? Besides the obvious fact he was an unfeeling beast, she had trouble classifying the man himself. His clothing was fashionable but nothing fancy, and the one-room cottage he called home told her little about him except that he was tidy and of modest means. Yet he spoke wellborn English and carried himself with an air of command.

No matter. Grayson would not find her an obedient captive. She planned to fight him every day, every hour, with every word and breath. She would find a way to escape.

With that in mind, she fled outside, only to discover Grayson had described her canyon jail aptly. The land was a mere strip hidden by a profusion of wild daffodils, primrose, and bluebells. Giant oak trees sheltered the hideaway from prying eyes by fanning the sky with their far-reaching branches. Ancient willows swayed with the wind, their leaves forming a wall of green at eye-level, convincing outsiders nothing lay below nature's color and finery.

The gate he had erected would indeed keep her trapped more than adequately. She stared up at its formidable height and the sharp stakes atop it protruding upward, dangerous and waiting.

She felt trapped. Her fists curled at her sides. How she resented Grayson, that knave! What would become of the perfect life she had planned? What would become of her?

Peering at the gate, she noted a hole just fit for a

key. Elation surged. Yes, she could escape. All she had
to do was find the key, for surely he possessed it. That
meant searching his belongings . . . and his person. Victoria rolled her eyes heavenward, praying for more
courage. How could she search him, touch him? She
couldn't fathom putting her hands on him during his
waking hours. He was arrogant enough to deem it an
invitation and virile enough to accept.

Dear God, what if she couldn't escape? She would be
forced to entertain his ultimatum. Though succumbing
to Grayson was bound to be less painful, the thought
of allowing a stranger into her bed was abhorrent. She
wouldn't take him as a lover, allowing him the intimacies one would a husband. Such disgrace was unthinkable!

Yet if she refused his attentions and struggled against
him, she would only cause herself pain. The hideous
image she conjured from his earlier description of the
act lingered. Besides, rebelling against a known killer
was something one didn't do unless one wanted to die.

He had her well tied in a quandary in which she had
little time to make up her mind, and he was using it to
his advantage.

Her only hope was defiance and escape, and she
swore she'd pursue them mercilessly.

After avoiding Victoria during her bath in the pond,
Dominic had seen her, fiery hair glistening, skin dewy,
return to the cottage again. His stomach rumbled, and
he knew he could not avoid the dwelling they shared
forever, despite the fact he found himself starving more
for the sight of her than food.

Shoving the thought aside, he strode for the cottage

and threw the door wide. Startled, Victoria whirled to face him, clad only in a sheet.

Sweet Jesus! Dominic gripped the door's latch between tight fingers, praying the vision before him would vanish.

She reminded him of a Grecian goddess—wrapped in white, pure, compelling . . . damning. His impulsive fingers itched to snatch away the sheet covering her. Her auburn hair tumbled over one shoulder and nipped at her narrow waist.

The urge to tousle her in that sheet kicked him in the gut. He wanted to see her indigo eyes darken to dark pools of desire before she pulsed around him in satisfaction.

But she hated him.

Dominic redirected his stare and shook his regret away.

Aristocratic women were simply dangerous. They passed the art of deception down from generation to generation, quietly destroying the lives of unsuspecting men foolish enough to crave their nearness. Hadn't Marcella taught him that well enough?

As he crossed the cottage, his captive backed away from him. The sheet covering her swayed about her bare calves. Dominic felt another unwanted surge of desire pulse through his belly. Thick and hot, the ache settled in his loins.

He took another step toward her, watching her eyes grow wider and warier The thought that she regarded him as little more than a monster twisted something within his chest, despite the fact he had strived to give her that very impression.

Dominic shook himself from his wayward thoughts. "Get dressed."

Victoria shot him a defiant glare, then turned to her satchel. He retreated outside.

Cursing, he shoved his fingers through his hair. *Focus, focus,* he demanded of himself—only to find Victoria's accusing visage lurking in his mind.

She hated him, just as he'd plotted. Christ, why did it bother him? And why, after months of planning, had he hesitated before telling her of his plans to bed her? No, rape her, he corrected himself. With the ill-feelings she held for him now, he needed no great intellect to realize the House of Stuart would rule England again before she would come to his bed willingly.

But raping Victoria seemed unconscionable, unthinkable now that he realized she was more than a pawn in his scheme; she was a human being. How could he violate an innocent girl caught in the cross fire of his hatred for Phillip? Debase the maiden he'd forced himself to hurl vile threats at while she trembled and stared in horror with those large, liquid eyes? Hurt a woman he wanted to protect from Phillip, against all logic?

Sinking against the cottage's outside wall with a long sigh, Dominic wondered what had ever made him believe this crazed plot would avenge his Marcella and his own captivity in one bold move and free his soul from the burdens of duty, hatred . . . and guilt.

Pure insanity. He felt like the lowest kind of beast.

But what if, a voice within him asked, instead of rape, he tried to awaken her?

He released a disgusted sigh. Whom was he fooling? Seduction meant courting moonlight, fair skin, and soft kisses. Such a dance with temptation was dangerous, too much so.

Dominic wasn't naive; he knew his weaknesses, and

his unexpected desire for Victoria was one of them. To awaken her would mean awakening himself, confessing his want, revealing his own need—and leaving him vulnerable in a way he'd sworn he'd never be again.

With a grunt and a tug, Victoria settled her dress into place. She had never before thought it displayed too much bosom, but now felt acutely aware of the skin exposed for Grayson's view.

Determined to ignore her dress—and him—she retrieved her brush, then stood before the small mirror above Grayson's washstand to fix her hair. Lord, she looked hideous! A garish purple-green bruise flared at her temple and over her eyebrow where she had fallen. The mass of her red hair was in shambles. Only the curls around her face softened the image. She pinched her cheeks and was rewarded with a bloom of color.

Oh, why did she care how she looked anyway? She thrust the brush furiously through her hair. It wasn't as if she wanted Grayson to find her attractive. He was beastly. He was unforgivably crude!

But he was also sinfully handsome and somehow made her pulse pound faster at his nearness.

Thinking like that was nothing short of foolish. No matter what he made her feel, she would not allow him to tumble her in the name of revenge. She just wanted to return to the duke of Dalmont, the marriage they had arranged, and the certainty her future would be happy.

The hours passed; a still blackness fell across the sky. The cold, humid air left Victoria feeling unsettled. Edgy and restless, she paced until she heard the metal latch lift on the cottage's heavy door. She glanced up to see Grayson enter.

The cottage suddenly seemed smaller and warmer.

Without a word, he doffed his shirt and draped it across the back of the cherry rocker. As he moved, Victoria watched the play of his muscles and golden skin across his shoulder blades.

Absently, he touched his chest, his flat palm stretching over hard muscle. Mesmerized, she watched his hand glide across taut, satiny skin.

The man didn't have any modesty, Victoria decided as her face suffused with hot color.

Do women caress their lovers that way? another forbidden voice inside her asked. Horrified, she dismissed the question.

"Have you eaten?" he offered.

"No." She turned away, chiding herself for seeing him as anything more than a blackguard. "I don't have an appetite."

He strode to her, a challenging glint in his eyes that did not bode well, and grasped her shoulders.

"Why do you turn away from me? Do you think yourself so beautiful I can scarcely keep my hands off you?"

He was too near, his presence too powerful. Victoria tried to pull away, to control her uneven breathing. Grayson held on, not allowing her to retreat.

"I—I . . . No."

No? She was a fool. Though confident in her appeal, Marcella had oft complained that her dark eyes were drab. She had whined that her breasts weren't full enough. Victoria had neither of those problems. And if Marcella could have seen Victoria, she would have clawed his captive's eyes out in jealousy. Why couldn't Victoria have been plain? Christ, he didn't need to be tempted now, especially by her.

Fingers shaking, he thrust her away as quickly as he

had captured her and stalked across the room. "You have nothing to fear from me for the next three days, dear lady. Until then, I've no plans to touch you."

"I don't fear you in the least," she retorted.

He raised a jet brow in challenge. "Then why do you jump each time I cast my gaze upon you?"

She marched up to him, her face inches from his. "Maybe you're so homely I can barely stand to look upon you."

Grayson laughed but voiced no response, so Victoria turned away. Grabbing her brush off the ancient washstand, she raked it through her hair. As she braided the curly mass, she became aware of Grayson's stare. Across the cottage, she perceived him watching her, studying her.

"Come here." His deep voice resonated across the room as he sat in a chair before the hearth.

Refusing to look in his direction, she shook her head. Heat flooded her.

"Come here," he repeated. "Or are you afraid?"

Victoria hesitated. Then mustering her bravado, she rose and paced forward, determined to prove he didn't intimidate her.

"That's it," he whispered. "Closer."

She halted an arm's length from him. "What do you want?"

"If you're not afraid, does it matter? A trifle closer."

She crept another step toward him.

"One more step, my lady."

His voice dropped to a whisper; the effect was hypnotic. With each step, she resented the spellbinding power of that velvety voice. Again, she shuffled forward. Mere inches separated them.

He took her hand. She tried to pull from his grasp—

until he began stroking her palm with his thumb, freezing her with tingles of sensation.

Her gaze rapt, she stared at his dark face, into his hot, knowing eyes.

"If you find me so ugly. Why do you stare?"

"I—I . . ." she stammered, betraying her suddenly hot cheeks.

A smile curved his lips upward. The feather-light touch of his fingers teased their way up the bare inside of her arm. His touch shot shocking heat from her center through her limbs. The drumbeat of her pulse erupted into a march.

"What if I were to kiss you? Put my hands to your woman's flesh?"

Gasping, she recoiled, trying to wrench from his grasp. "I won't let you defile me."

His grip tightened, and he tugged on her arm until she fell into his lap. He captured her wrists and forced her palms flat against his naked chest.

Springy curls coiled around her fingers. The heat of his skin startled the anger out of her, jolted her into awareness of his heartbeat beneath her fingertips, of his earthy scent. He brought her face within inches of his, where she could do nothing but stare.

"Am I so ugly you cannot tear your gaze away?" he taunted.

He mocked her, the swine! Scrambling to find her feet, Victoria struggled to make her way off his lap. Instead, he bound her there with a steely grip upon her thighs.

Of its own volition, her gaze made its way back to his face. Square and abrupt, the authoritative jawline served to make Grayson intriguing. No, if she were honest, he was incredibly handsome.

Her pulse soared as she stared at him. Why was she so aware of the heat and woodsy scent rising from his skin?

"Go on; you were curious enough to stare. Touch me," he invited, his voice smooth as brandy.

Her fingers curled around his wrists, her nails digging in. "I have merely memorized your face so I could describe it to anyone willing to hunt you down and hang you!"

Grayson laughed, his eyes warm and glittering.

Tilting her chin upward, Victoria scowled and refused to give the devil the satisfaction of admitting he fascinated her.

"I would say that I'd prefer to rot in hell, but I think I'm already there. And you must be Satan himself," she cried. "I would allow a thousand other men into my bed before I'd let you in!"

The smile slid off his face, replaced by an icy glare. "Doubtless you would. But there won't be *anyone* except me, my lady. That I promise you."

Four

Footsteps crunching gravel outside the cottage awoke Victoria. She sat up in bed when, to her shock, she heard two men conversing, the words low, unintelligible. One voice, deep and intriguing, she knew as Grayson's. The other she did not recognize.

The strength of the voices grew as they approached, until the men stopped just outside.

Hope and curiosity mingled within her as she crept from the bed toward the shuttered window. Silently, she paused beneath, praying Grayson would say something that would clue her about their location or aid her escape. Certainly, he would not volunteer information.

"Do you have news?" Grayson asked the stranger.

"Imagine our friend Dalmont's surprise when he awoke on the morn of his wedding to find his bride abducted." The stranger laughed. "To say he was angry would be mild, indeed."

Grayson chuckled, the sound richer than burgundy wine. Her stomach fluttered with an unnamed emotion.

"What did he do?" Dominic asked.

"Besides curse so violently it gave the servants pause? I believe he reviled the swine who sired you, then, predictably, vowed revenge."

"Which is indeed sweet," Grayson declared with a laugh. "What followed?"

"Once Dalmont recovered from his attack of the vapors, he contacted his chum Lord Gaphard."

"The Upper Magistrate?"

"That very one," the stranger confirmed. "Then he declared you the lady's abductor."

"I expected something of the sort."

He expected the law to come down around his ears? Grayson was a very dangerous man, no question. And he sounded so calm, as if crime were a way of life to him. Perhaps it was.

"Lord Gaphard is more convinced than ever of your guilt, Dominic. He swore to report to the Old Bailey and demand your death. Immediately," the stranger said.

Dominic paused. "That brings no surprises, either."

"Do not forget Lord Gaphard is a very powerful man," the stranger warned. "He has friends close to the Crown."

"I would have died in prison," Dominic countered, a sudden vehemence in his voice. "If the jackals at Newgate had not executed me, they would have soon starved or beaten me to death. At least this way, with Lady Victoria, I have a chance to complete my revenge."

"So we hope. However, Dalmont has hired a band of cutthroats to search for you two. A more vicious bunch of culls I've never seen," the stranger warned.

"Let them search. In fact, I invite it."

"If they find you, do you imagine they will waste the effort to drag you back to Newgate, where you might rot for months again? Dalmont will not take that chance. He'll see you dead, make no mistake."

"Rely on the false clues you and I left to lead Phillip

in the wrong direction." Dominic paused. "As for Lord Gaphard and good King George, I have to believe that I will somehow prove Phillip murdered Marcella, hopefully before I'm captured."

Victoria bit her lip to hold in her gasp. Dear Lord, was it possible her intended had participated in the murder of a woman? Was the duke of Dalmont capable of such a heinous act? Her memory replayed snatches of the conversation she'd overheard in his garden. He'd thought the woman a whore and ordered Dominic's murder without pause. The inkling of doubts swirling within Victoria left her confused and disquieted.

"Where have Phillip's men searched?" her captor asked.

"They scoured the docks in London first, fearing you'd flee England with Lady Victoria. When that proved fruitless, they moved west through Wiltshire to Somerset and began following our clues."

"Perfect. But we must be prepared in case Phillip's men shift toward us. Can you stay close to his town house?" After a moment's pause, Dominic continued. "Find out whatever you can and come back in a few weeks."

"Consider it done, friend," the stranger answered.

"You have my thanks."

"I've always known you were wrongly accused and felt proud to help in righting that wrong accusation."

"Someday that may come to pass." Grayson's voice carried no conviction.

If Dalmont were guilty of Marcella's murder, then Grayson must be innocent. Was it possible? Her captor claimed to be without guilt, and the stranger clearly accepted that as fact. Did she believe Dominic Grayson capable of cold-blooded murder? That question wasn't as easily answered. She wanted to believe he wasn't, for her safety if nothing else, and yet . . . he had abducted her, ruthlessly disregarding her protests, then threatened rape.

Confusion swelled within her, crowding out logic. The few facts she possessed did not fit together, like pieces of a puzzle larger and more sinister than she was capable of assembling. And Victoria had a suspicion she was missing a few parts.

The stranger changed the subject. "Have you carried forth with all your plans?"

After a tense, silent pause, Grayson replied, "Are you asking if I've bedded Lady Victoria?"

"Since it's clear you were successful in abducting her, I suppose I am."

"I would prefer not to speak of it."

The other man sighed. "Dominic, do you think violating an innocent girl will bring Marcella back?"

"Do you expect me to disregard Marcella's death and dishonor?" Dominic's low voice boomed.

"Of course not, but do you truly believe you'll be vindicated by stealing Lady Victoria's virginity?"

Dominic paused. "If you disapprove of my intentions, then go. You know the way out."

"My approval is hardly the point. I simply wish you to see the consequences. This plan won't change your status with the Crown. If anything, this scheme makes you more nefarious."

"I could *not* sit passively while Phillip went on with his plans to marry. Besides, if Victoria had wed Phillip, I shudder to imagine the wretched life she would have led and the death that would have eventually followed."

"So take her under your wing, and not into your bed."

"I've made my plans. As I said, if you disapprove, leave."

The stranger sighed wearily. "Dominic, you know I will stay. I was simply trying to make you see logic."

"If you're hungry, I have fruit and bread," he said, an obvious ploy to change the subject.

"So you won't consider it?" the stranger pressed.

Victoria held her breath, hoping her captor had been swayed.

"Phillip will pay for everything. And she is the key."

Minutes after Victoria finished dressing, Dominic returned with the stranger in tow. She faced them, her gaze assessing the other man.

He was nearly as tall as Grayson, though somewhat less broad. Victoria guessed the stranger might be Grayson's junior by a year, perhaps two. Then the man smiled. She returned the smile, knowing he had some sympathy for her plight. Right now, he was her best hope for freedom.

"My lady, this is Andrew. He will be with us from time to time." Grayson turned to the other man. "My friend, meet Lady Victoria Tarrent."

With a gallant smile, Andrew lifted her hand to his lips. "Such a pleasure to meet you, Lady Victoria."

Shooting him a bright smile in return, she greeted him. "How do you do, sir?"

"Sir?" He laughed. "No, that will not do. Much too formal. I insist you call me Andrew."

Victoria opened her mouth to insist it was too soon for the familiarity of first names, then glimpsed Grayson's expression. Irritation stamped itself on his face in the form of a narrow-eyed scowl. Though she had no idea why Andrew's suggestion would vex

Grayson, the opportunity to needle him in whatever small way she could proved too great.

"I'm very honored to meet you, Andrew."

"No more honored than I," he assured, his voice low.

Victoria cast a clandestine glance at her captor. He looked stiff as stone, from his pursed lips to furrowed brow. She paused to wonder at her anger, then decided to enjoy it instead. With that, she threaded her arm through Andrew's, sent him a glowing grin, and followed him into the cottage.

Across the small, battered table, Victoria studied the two men with whom she sat, so different from each other. Though she knew little of Andrew, she had hope she could persuade him to help her escape.

Silently, she finished the vegetables on her plate, making occasional eye contact with Andrew. *Help me,* her gaze implored as she nibbled on dark bread. She cheered silently when his sympathetic gaze turned her way.

Pushing aside her half-full plate, she whispered, "Excuse me," injecting her small voice with despondency.

Andrew stood as she did. Grayson remained seated, arching a cynical brow—which she ignored. She cast a dejected glance over her shoulder, one she prayed would further rouse Andrew's sympathy, then let herself out of the cottage.

Ten minutes of tense silence passed inside the cabin. Dominic studied Andrew's agitated expressions. Another ten minutes ticked by. Andrew's gaze repeatedly darted to the door, concern mapped across his tawny face.

Sighing, he finally set his napkin on the table. "She's been gone too long."

Slouching in his chair, Dominic raised a questioning brow.

"I hope she's come to no harm. Perhaps I should check on her," Andrew offered.

Dominic toyed with the stem of his wineglass. "You're aware, of course, that is exactly what she wants."

Andrew looked across the table in puzzlement. "What gives you such an impression?"

"I've spent hours watching her, my friend. I can read the expression on her face. I know that forlorn look she cast you was not entirely genuine."

Andrew frowned. "Be easy on her, Dominic. She has every reason to feel forlorn."

Dominic shrugged, then drained the contents of his wineglass in one long swallow. The wench meant nothing to him. "Go find her if it will ease your mind."

"Thank you," Andrew replied with a stiff nod. "I want to be certain she is well."

"But before you go, appease my curiosity." Dominic watched Andrew across the table. "When did you become Victoria's protector? After you saw her bright smile? Are you hoping that if you're kind, she will let you bed her?"

Andrew frowned. "I merely seek to comfort her."

Dominic leaned across the table, eyes as dangerous as the anger building in him. "I know your idea of comforting a woman, and I will not have it."

"God's blood, I had no thought of seducing the girl, just talking to her," he defended.

"You've never thought of a woman as anything other than a warm being to pleasure you." Dominic rose, and his anger did the same as his hard gaze pinned Andrew in his seat. "If you're hoping to bed Victoria, forget it. You will not touch her."

Andrew stood slowly, his mouth agape. "What is this? Jealousy?" He laughed. "Does the thought of another man's hands on her beautiful body disturb you?"

Yes! something within Dominic shouted. He struggled to silence it. Jealousy he did not need. It banished logic; it invited chaos. Did Victoria find Andrew attractive? He lost his appetite pondering that question. The knots in his belly were still lodged in place, twisting and tangling his insides. Why? What was it about her that wouldn't leave him in peace?

"Don't assume Lady Victoria will behave as Lady Marcella," Andrew said.

His scarred heart burst forth a well of rage. "That is enough!"

"Not by half," Andrew countered. "You cannot punish your captive for Marcella's sins."

"Thank you for reminding me that my wife cuckolded me." Dominic's voice was tight and brittle.

"I've no need to, since you never let yourself forget."

Dominic whirled away, taking deep breaths to ebb the rising tide of anguish. Andrew was right. He had never forgotten or forgiven Marcella's betrayal with his friend. He had never wanted the wound to heal. He had let it fester, hoping the pain would prevent him from repeating the mistake of trusting a woman.

He pushed away from the table and crossed to the fireplace. Resting his foot on the hearth, he braced his forearm on the mantle. "Soon, I will need those favors you said I could count on. Beware of developing sentiments for Victoria."

"I suggest you listen to your own bloody advice," Andrew retorted, then strode to the door, slamming it behind him.

* * *

Victoria sat at the edge of the pond, listening to the rush of the waterfall, considering her plan. Ten minutes ago, she'd given up hope that Andrew was coming after her. Perhaps she'd only imagined the sympathy in his eyes.

"You've been gone longer than I expected," Andrew said, suddenly beside her. Startled, she jumped as he sat down. "I grew concerned for your safety."

Victoria felt a rush of triumph. Perhaps something of her plan had worked, after all. "Thank you, but I'm much safer here than inside with that beast."

Andrew sighed. "He is a . . . difficult man. Those who knew him in years past say he has changed."

That was hardly the information she had hoped for. She didn't want to care for the man he had been, or the plights he had suffered. She should focus solely on escape.

Victoria sighed with frustration. "Do you think Grayson is justified in seeking revenge?"

After a pause, he replied, "Honor demands such; however, I would use another method. But I'm soft-hearted. Dominic is not. Perhaps Newgate did that to him." Andrew shrugged. "To me, using you is unacceptable. To Dominic, his vengeance is most important. He would sacrifice anything to have it."

Victoria expected such determination from a soulless man like Grayson, but Andrew's words did not hearten her. "What am I to do?" she implored. "Surely there must be something, some way. . . ."

The breeze kicked up, whipping soft, russet hair across her cheek. Andrew touched the wayward strands, then placed them behind her shoulder.

"My lady, Dominic is a mighty foe. He is stronger, his worldly experience wider. His anger is great, indeed.

Those facts alone should show you the folly of fighting him."

Victoria refused to let her hope sink. She turned imploring eyes to him. "Take me from here. Please. He's going to force me to—" She bit back the terrible words, unable to say them, lest they become true. "I cannot even repeat his vile plan."

Andrew looked away. A pained frown on his tawny face gave Victoria hope. "I vowed to Dominic I would not help you."

"He will ruin my life, ruin me," she argued, desperation heightening her voice. "Hurt me!"

"Not unless you refuse to cooperate. Even then I have doubts he will carry through with his threat."

"I have no such doubts."

Andrew bobbed his head in acknowledgment. "But you will be alive. That is more than can be said for . . ."

"For Marcella?" Victoria finished, sensing Andrew's hesitation to discuss Dominic's personal affairs.

Andrew's gaze honed in on her. "He told you of her?"

"A trifle." Victoria sighed, fear and frustration closing like a vise about her throat. "Hurting me will not change anything. Talk to him, please. Certainly you can make him see reason."

"I have tried."

"What are you suggesting I do? Wait for him to rape me?"

"Fighting him will gain you nothing." He sighed heavily. "But you will fight anyway." In a low tone, he advised, "Be careful. Remember, you play the mouse to his cat, and he can spring his trap on you anytime he wishes."

"Is there no way to escape?" she demanded in panic.

"There may be. If you find it, I shall be happy for you. Come," he said, standing. "We should go back inside. Dominic will be wondering where we are."

"And we mustn't keep him waiting long, else he will take his anger out on me. Is that right?"

Remorse dominated Andrew's gentle face. "Try not to judge him harshly, my lady. Perhaps his attitude will soften."

"Do not fill me with false hope. I know very little about Mr. Grayson, but I do know he's not likely to change his mind."

Andrew brought her hand to his lips. "With Dominic, you never know."

Five

As night descended, Victoria paced the cottage in agitation, feeling as if the dim, shuttered room shrank with each step.

Three days ago, Grayson had issued his ultimatum: Succumb to his lovemaking or be raped. What would she say? Surrender would likely cause her less pain, but cost too much in dignity and virtue. And now that this abduction had ruined her in society's eyes, what of her future if Grayson released her?

To add to her anxiety, the small hope she had harbored of Andrew's interceding on her behalf had died when he'd departed the previous morn.

Worse, she could not discount the probability that Dominic had murdered Marcella, despite the overheard conversation. She could well imagine that a persuasive man like her captor had convinced a trusting Andrew of his innocence.

She could not take a ruthless killer into her bed. True, she did not feel revulsion when Grayson was near. Oh no, she felt something more disturbing, more terrifying for the riot of trembling sensations he unleashed inside her.

Even if Grayson were innocent, Victoria's knowledge of what passed between a man and a woman was too minimal to rely upon with comfort. To confuse matters, she knew Dominic's interest in her was solely as a pawn, not a woman. In fact, he spent most of his days outdoors, out of her presence. He rose and left the cottage well before she woke. Only his folded blankets and empty coffee cup reminded her that he, too, inhabited the tiny cottage.

The door opened a moment later, accompanied by the night sounds of chirping crickets and croaking frogs. Victoria turned at the sound of Grayson entering. His presence filled the small, low-roofed room. She tingled with awareness.

Without a word, he dished out a helping of last night's stew, then offered Victoria a bowl. She declined and watched as he ate, feeling tension ripple through the air, clawing at her stomach.

Dear God, she prayed, let him forget his hideous ultimatum.

Under lowered lashes, Victoria watched Grayson clean his knife and fork, then lay the blade in his trunk.

"Ready yourself for bed, my lady." With a last, lingering glance, he exited.

Victoria stared at the trunk, struck by one sole realization: Grayson had neglected to lock the knife away. Her mind raced. Her heart thumped in her chest. She couldn't spare time to wonder why, not when she had so much to fight for.

She glanced again at the trunk and hesitated, knowing she could never stab Grayson or anyone else. That didn't matter. He only had to believe she would.

Palms damp, she dashed to the trunk and, with trembling fingers, lifted the lid. Staring at the gleaming blade, she reached for it and, without wasting another second, gripped the weapon by the hilt and shut the trunk.

Upon hearing Grayson's impatient steps outside pacing, she scurried across the room and hid the knife under her pillow. After rapidly disrobing, she donned a lawn dressing gown. No sooner had she finished than Dominic reentered the room. Victoria tried desperately to ignore him as she settled herself on the edge of the bed and brushed the length of her hair.

His footsteps sounded against the wooden floor, their rhythm pulsing dread within her as he crossed the room. Closer he came as she raked the brush through her auburn tresses nervously. Soon, he stood beside her. He did not touch her, but she felt him as surely as if he did.

"Victoria, your three days are over. I want your answer. Now."

As she twisted around, her gaze flew to his face. She flinched at his weighty but unreadable expression, then glanced at her pillow, remembering the knife underneath.

"Well?" he prodded.

His curt tone set her teeth on edge. In that instant, she knew she could never be his passive victim, even if it cost her her life.

"I will not lie beneath you like some helpless maiden and do nothing to save my dignity."

"I see." He stared at her for a motionless moment, his narrowed mouth and glittering eyes betraying his displeasure. "I want this over."

"Now?" Her mouth fell open as her mind exploded with shock.

In answer, he unfastened the two buttons topping the

front of his simple white shirt. "Why put off what is inevitable?"

Jerking the garment over his head, he turned to drape it across the back of the rocker . . . a silent white ghost portending her fate.

Victoria stared at the broad expanse of his bronzed back, then inched across the bed and lifted her pillow, wincing at the whisper of the sheets. As her palm closed around the steely hilt of the knife, a mantle of confidence enveloped her. She could thwart him.

As Dominic worked at the lacings of his breeches, she crept behind him. Heart pounding, she inched up on her toes and pressed the blade to his throat. "Release me, or I shall kill you."

To her surprise, her voice sounded loud and steady, but her hand quivered. The blade scraped his skin once . . . twice as she waited, breath held, for his reaction. His pulse pumped hard and steady against her hand. Moments ticked by; Grayson said nothing.

Suddenly, he tensed, capturing her wrist, and propelled the blade from his neck. He spun her around, wrenching the knife from her, and with a curse flung the weapon across the room. The clink of the blade startled her as it struck the wall, then clanged to the floor.

"How the hell did you get that?" he demanded, his eyes as damning as his raspy voice.

Victoria's eyes made an instinctive journey across the room, but she stubbornly said nothing.

"Damn, the trunk." With a curse, he shook his head and trod across the floor, mumbling something about carelessness before grabbing the knife. Not sparing her a glance, he locked the blade away.

"You will not escape. I cannot let you." He crossed

the cottage to stand before her again, taking her shoulders in his grip.

"But—"

"Stay here and resign yourself to your damned choice."

"I won't," she shot back, equally determined.

He advanced; she retreated from his grasp until her back hugged the wall. Her stomach fell to her knees when she realized she'd maneuvered herself into a trap.

"My time for revenge has come, Victoria."

She wrenched her gaze away from the raw power of his bare chest to the door, intending to run. His arms encircled her waist, capturing her. He backed her against the bed. As he leaned into her, she fell to the mattress, quivering. Dominic pinioned her wrists above her head with one hand. With the large, shaking fingers of his other hand, he tried unfastening her tiny alabaster buttons, without success.

Victoria's panicked mind registered the sounds of a guttural oath followed by fabric ripping. She renewed her fight, kicking and biting him. He had her well contained. Within seconds, the thin garment joined his shirt on the floor. That instant, that easily, he stripped her naked.

She kicked and thrashed and yelled. Dominic threw his thigh over hers, further trapping her. She hurled curses his way, then sank her teeth into his shoulder. Wincing against the pain of her sharp teeth, Dominic cast her a dark glare . . .

And he saw tears sliding down her face, wetting the pale perfection of her cold cheeks. Willing himself to put the sight out of his mind, Dominic slid down her body. Her skin burned icy hot against his everywhere they touched. He felt her body, tense and rigid, pressing into the mattress. Ignoring the sensations, the encroaching distaste of this task, he wedged a knee between hers.

Revenge, he reminded himself mercilessly. Phillip had never had a second thought about bedding Marcella. *Yes, but Marcella had been willing . . .*

Dominic's stomach bucked; he swallowed the bile and dropped his hand to the lacings of his breeches.

"No!" Victoria screamed her denial of his invasion.

Compelled, he looked down at her face, at her desperate, ravaged expression. Those blue eyes, so beautiful with a smile, glowed red-rimmed and wide in her chalky face, making her seem a mere ghost of herself. That, coupled with her tangled hair and nearly white lips, crushed his determination.

He couldn't hurt her like this, no matter how much revenge demanded satisfaction.

This damage would be his doing and, once done, could never be repaired. No matter how neatly he rationalized it, this violation of her body would cause her pain forever. He was not a murderer, nor had he become a rapist.

The adrenaline pumping through him at the thought of imminent revenge evaporated along with his rage. He felt violent, vile.

He stilled, holding her shaking form against him, hating himself for the tremors that rocked her body. Somehow, he would avenge Marcella's seduction with an eye for an eye, awaken Victoria gently, the way an untried maid should be. Then could he keep both his revenge and his conscience in harmony.

Any emotions a seduction evoked would simply have to be quelled, ruthlessly. It would not do to want Victoria too much.

"I could have stripped your virginity in an instant," he said, voice hoarse. "I know that is not what you wish."

Fresh tears trickled from her blue wet eyes. "Damn you, of course not!"

"Then bloody well change your mind." His voice pleaded where his words did not. "Let me try to pleasure you."

She struggled again, raking her fingernails across his cheek. He said nothing when she drew blood.

Victoria averted her gaze from his burning eyes, desperate not to show any more of her tears. He would only interpret them as surrender.

"Victoria, look at me." When she did not respond, he stroked a gentle hand across her cheek. "Please."

His use of the word "please," coupled with his shockingly soft touch, intrigued her enough to look at him.

"I wanted you to know what rape would feel like." His words hung in the air, oddly raspy, as his heart beat in rapid staccato against her. His bare skin felt slick and warm and steely-soft against her own.

"You bastard!" She clawed beneath him for freedom.

He rose slowly from the bed, covered her with the blanket, then turned away to lace his breeches. His lack of response stung almost as much as his intention.

"How could you— strip me so brutally? How could you touch me like that?" she demanded.

Turning to her with an expression that looked oddly like regret, he whispered, "I do not wish you harm, my lady. I can only vow I shall use the gentlest touch to give you pleasure."

Doubt and fear clashed within Victoria. She wondered about the tingling that usually assailed her when he watched her with those arresting hazel eyes. Would his lovemaking ever feel like that? Or would she feel violated, as she had moments ago?

Indecision scattered her logic into a thousand mismatched puzzle pieces. She clutched the blanket to her chest.

"How will *this* vindicate you?" she demanded. "If I give my nod to this indecent agreement, what will it accomplish?"

He retrieved his discarded shirt. "It is the only way I can achieve revenge."

"And how many times will I be expected to grace your bed?"

With a resigned sigh, he raked a hand through his hair. "I had thought to keep you as a mistress for six months." He stared long and intently, as if measuring his words. "Now I will accept just once."

"O—once," she stammered.

"Do we have an arrangement?" he questioned, eyes probing.

Victoria paused. Certainly once, in any form or fashion, would be better than six months of servitude, where he might take her anytime, day or night, at his discretion. Wouldn't it?

"If you agree to my condition," she said finally.

He nodded. "I'm listening."

As she groped for the right words, embarrassment flooded her, along with a strange liquid heat. She kept her eyes riveted to the blanket covering her. "That our *once* does not happen now."

His expression was curiously sad. "You act as cheerful as a condemned man meeting his executioner. Not that I blame you, for you can have little concept of how fulfilling lovemaking is."

"There was nothing fulfilling in—"

"Rape is meant to take. Desire is meant to give. With it, I could give you tenderness, a soft hand on your shoulder, a gentle kiss on your neck. A warm rush of shared breath as we—"

"You've yet to answer me," Victoria cut in, ending his provocative statement that had made her stomach tighten with the dangerous feeling she felt too often around him. "Do you agree to the condition?"

His gaze touched her face, seeming to reach within her. "If you come to my bed willingly, I shall wait until you're ready."

Victoria rose minutes after the sun to find Grayson gone, his blankets folded fastidiously on the couch.

Dear God, what had she agreed to in last night's shadows? She had sworn to willingly bare her body. In day's glaring light, she held no illusions—he expected a passionate response.

Impossible.

Wasn't it? After all, how could she feel desire for a man who had ruined her plans to wed, carried her off to a remote cottage, and threatened her bodily. A man accused of murder.

Rising from the bed, Victoria sought a dress and her hairbrush. While struggling into her clothes, she wondered if he had possibly been accused unjustly. Such was not uncommon, though she doubted the duke of Dalmont could be guilty of Marcella's murder. Then why revenge? Grayson felt using her was his only way to strike back, though he had not seized the opportunity to rape her when she'd been naked beneath him. Some measure of sanity or goodness must have stopped him from the violation, though he clearly believed it was to his benefit. Was that the kind of man who beat his lover to death?

She shook her head to clear it. Even if, beneath his gruff exterior, lay the heart of a saint, could she bed down with him? From what little she knew, she feared he would demand total surrender, the kind that encompassed not only her body, but her soul. He didn't seem the kind of man to settle for anything done in half measure.

Raking a brush through her hair, she decided she wouldn't have to. He had agreed, after all, to wait until she was ready. As far as she was concerned, he could wait until the Red Sea parted again. She could ignore that unsettling spark he ignited within her.

Grayson opened the door and entered the cottage, interrupting her reverie. He cast her a stare tinged with desire and challenge before dropping into a chair. Sipping from a tin cup, he studied her over the rim with that same gaze.

"Good morning, my lady," he greeted her, his full lips curling up into a devastating smile that threw her off base even as it warmed the pit of her stomach. He looked approachable, almost boyish . . . and utterly male.

"If you say," she snapped, determined to deny his smile's effect on her.

His grin deepened, displaying the dimple in his chin. "Would your disposition improve with breakfast, my lady?"

"My disposition will only improve with my freedom!"

"I fear I am in for much of your ill temper then." He raised a mischievous brow. "Those frowns on such a beautiful face are disheartening, indeed."

Victoria stared at him suspiciously. He no more

wanted to exchange pleasantries than your average baron with his servant. Nor was the reason for his change in temperament hard to discern. He wanted to charm his way under her sheets. The blackguard. The knave! Grayson had the nerve of ten men—with more to spare.

"I will not fall willingly into your bed because you say a few pleasing words."

His expression was all innocence. "I had merely imagined that, after last night's agreement, we had no further need to be enemies."

Victoria shot him a withering glare. "Your imagination is nearly as inflated as your opinion of yourself."

He cleared his throat. "What did you do at home for fun? Kick the family pet?"

"Of course not." She frowned. "Birdie I could love easily. He never dragged me from my bed in the rain and kept me from my betrothed."

He frowned. "You had a bird as a pet?"

"No, Birdie is a dog."

"Birdie is a dog?" Much as she hated to admit it, he looked charmingly confused. "Would you name your cat *Mousey?*"

Holding back a laugh, she settled for a rueful smile. "We got Birdie when I was learning to talk. Mother told me I was a trifle . . . confused about animals."

"Ah. Do you miss Birdie?"

His soft question made a sharp gash in the wall holding her emotions within. Memories trickled out, of Wilton House and its gardens, her parents and the strong bond of their love, of her friends, and of Birdie. All made her ache with longing.

"I miss him terribly, not that you care."

Grayson said nothing at first, but merely crossed the

room to her with slow steps. His eyes traveled the length of her body once, twice. Victoria felt her blood heat in response to the hunger naked in his gaze.

"I do care. I know this captivity has not been easy for you."

His gentle understanding, to say nothing of his velvety voice, sent shivers scattering through her. Victoria swallowed, fighting to control her wobbling knees.

Why did she respond to him with anything other than fear and loathing? Certainly she wasn't daft enough to want his good opinion or his company. She shouldn't care if he had a good side.

Though it made her a fool of the first order, she did care.

"I am sorry," he whispered.

His fingers curled around her wrist, his warm touch seeping into her, sending her heart into a pumping frenzy. She tried to twist away, but he drew her forward until her breasts nestled against him, shocking her with an instant of heat—and unearthing a surge of wants. The solid masculinity of his shoulders towered above her, the power of his chest enveloping her.

These thoughts were nothing short of insanity, his attempt at seduction, his hope to bed her without resistance.

"No," she argued, voice breathy. "You want only revenge."

He gentled; his free hand rose to her hair, stunning her into silence as he touched the copper strands, handling her with the care reserved for a babe as he coiled them around his fingers. As he drew out the tortoiseshell combs, his eyes widened in awe when the heavy curls fell around her in a tumble. He slid his fingers into her tresses.

Victoria swallowed hard, unable to say a word.

Certainly he found touching her nothing more than an amusing game. But his glittering eyes seemed to ask for her touch, her very soul. Her own soul answered, *Yes, touch me.* The way he held her, as if he had been craving the feel of her, sent her self-control reeling. Victoria struggled to ignore the sensations, finding she could no more do so than she could block out the beat of her trumpeting heart.

She heard the nervous quickening of her breath. When his gaze fell to her mouth, she knew he was aware of it, too. His stare lingered there. Her lips tingled. She willed herself to turn away from his gaze, but his hands, anchored in her hair, brought her face back, a breath beneath his.

"Don't." Her barely audible word hung between them.

"You've no wish for pleasure?"

She had no answer to that. Even if she had, her tongue lay useless and thick within her mouth, tightly bound by the tingling sensations of her body.

"Stop," she whispered finally.

"Does my touch feel bad, love?"

His intimate whisper arced both pleasure and uncertainty through her. *Please, God, let this stop before he makes a fool of me.* Insidiously, a secret part of her wished Grayson's tenderness would stretch through eternity. "I do not like it."

She pushed her hands against his chest. In answer to her protest, Grayson moved to clasp her damp palm in his, squeezing gently on her hand. Disconcerted, Victoria wriggled her hand from his grasp, but her will seeped away as his thumb stroked her forefinger. In the pit of her stomach, a pulsing pleasure began.

She held her gaze to the floor, silently willing him to stop. His touch felt good—and dangerous. *Move away,* she ordered herself. She stood still as his free hand stroked her jawline, drifted down her arm, then wandered to her waist. Darts of sensation pierced her resolve.

"Stop this now. I cannot breathe," she whispered.

"Why not?"

"It . . ." She struggled to form words as a mist of unruly, shocking wants descended over her logic. "I feel odd."

"A tingle, perhaps?"

Of its own will, her head dropped back. Her gaze met the full curve of his mouth. Definitely a tingle. "Of course not."

He smiled at her lie, a flash of white teeth and charm. "You will feel more of that when I make love to you."

Settling his palms against the back of her head, Dominic sidled closer until his hard thighs bracketed her own. The tingles in her body multiplied when she inhaled his subtle woodsy scent, felt his warm exhalations on her mouth. Their gazes locked. His hazel eyes devoured her with a hungry, feral stare.

"Let me kiss you," he murmured.

Her knees went liquid at his words, as he slid his hands about her neck and tilted her face up to his. Dominic stroked her cheek, and Victoria knew an insane urge to melt against him.

Her breath lodged in her chest as she tried to shake her head, tried to seek good sense and reason. But his gaze was too compelling; his words, his touch, too seductive.

She watched him in a haze, felt his warm breath caress her lips. Drawing in a shaky breath as he inched closer, she surrendered to her yearning for the sensual persuasion of his mouth, for the heat his gaze promised so boldly. Her eyes slid shut; every muscle of her body strained to meet him, feel him.

His lips touched hers, softly at first. A gentle caress, nothing hurried, no demands. Exactly what she never expected of him. Exactly what her body craved.

His lips claimed hers again in soft possession. All breath and rational thought fled Victoria's mind as the tingles Dominic promised leapt through her body, centering in the pit of her belly. All thought dissipated except how exquisite this touch was, so unlike the violence of the day before . . . so perfect.

As Dominic groaned against her mouth, Victoria sank farther into his embrace, reveling in the feel of his callused palm sliding down her back. Her own arms found their way about his shoulders and clung.

At that, Dominic turned up the fire in his kiss, his mouth pliant, stroking . . . pleading for more. Gone were both her ability to think and breathe. Thick molten desire coiled through Victoria's body, even as her soul welcomed his sensual onslaught.

Dominic followed that kiss with another that demanded pleasure yet gave in equal measure. She clung tighter, living in the moment, never wanting it to end. Their fingers locked together; the warmth of his palm seared her own as she gathered him against her tighter, wanting, needing. Desire echoed the fire of his mouth, burning her lips as she returned the kiss.

Beneath her taut-fingered hands, she felt the tension bunch in his hard muscles. The scents of coffee, warm sun, and male musk touched her senses until she knew nothing but him.

She moved restlessly against him, wanting more. His

hand tightened at the small of her back, making her aware for the first time of his arousal. The female within her responded instinctively, the primal vibration of need beating like a native's drum.

Her rational mind protested from somewhere far away. Her awakened body refused to hear with the feel of his hard chest beneath her fingertips and the rightness of Dominic's male body flush against her own.

He touched her shoulder before delving downward, beneath her clothing. His palm closed over her breast, his thumb making a slow, aching trek across her tightened nipple. Hot, cold, desire, need—all came together in a flash as his hand encompassed her.

"It can be good, Victoria," he murmured on a moan. "Let me make love to you."

The press of his words, along with the unfamiliar heat of his fingers on her breasts, lifted Victoria out of her fog of desire long enough to be shocked by the liberties she'd permitted. She wrenched from his embrace.

Righting her bodice, she stared with accusing eyes. "Enough!"

He stepped away, jaw tense, drawing his hands from her body to his side. "As you wish."

Struggling to catch her breath, Victoria stared at him in growing anger. How easily she'd allowed him to touch her. How easily he had made her melt. How fully he'd manipulated her.

"Were you not content to abduct me, keep me from my betrothed and my future, then nearly rape me?" She shook her head angrily. "Must you trifle with me as well?"

Casting her a sharp glare, he panted, "It isn't as if you have no defenses. You have feminine wiles aplenty and more beauty to go with them."

"What do you speak of? Wiles?"

"All women have them," he said flatly. "It is the nature of the beast."

Did he genuinely believe that? If so, had Marcella taught him that lesson? "I hardly amuse myself by luring men in."

He hesitated, his face as tumultuous as the sky during a windstorm. She could read only disbelief. "If you say."

"I do say," she defended. "I would never lure in lovers to use them for my selfish purposes. I leave that ugly task to you."

She strode past him, a mere breath away, triumphant. Then his natural scent filtered into her consciousness. The heat of his body, stiff now to match his glare, penetrated next. That warm musk sent an unwelcome thrill through her, a thrill that jolted her with resentment as she left the cottage.

Victoria didn't like him, could never love him. How could he create the ache within her body she feared only he could ease?

Two nights later, Victoria woke from her troubled sleep to tangled sheets and semi-darkness. She thought first of Dominic's kiss. The ache in her belly hadn't eased, not with his constant proximity and blistering stares. If a kiss could conjure up this biting desire, what kind of tumult would a night in his bed bring?

Worse, her once-firm belief that he had murdered Marcella in cold blood now seemed hopelessly mired in a tangle of desire and doubts.

She could scarcely believe the gentle fingers that cradled her had beat Marcella to death. True, when Dominic talked with Andrew, he'd claimed he hadn't killed Marcella, and Andrew clearly accepted that. But was it illusion or fact? Victoria shook her head, not knowing what to believe.

Dear God, she needed to escape. Before she lost her sanity. Before she threw away her future and dishonored her family over an inexplicable passion. Before she gave her heart to a possible killer.

What about escaping now? She glanced over at Dominic's prone form, illuminated by a dying fire, sprawled on the floor. His clothes lay beside him, likely harboring the elusive key to the gate barring her freedom.

Creeping out of bed, across the cottage, she stopped before him as he slept on, unaware of her gaze.

Sleep softened his face. He looked almost at peace, but not quite. She wondered who or what had taken that from him. The resolution remained around those predatory eyes, the firm line of his full mouth, the taut power of his naked chest.

He had discarded his thin blanket sometime during the warm spring night. He wore only his short white drawers, which exposed everything below his knees and above his waist. With shameful curiosity, she gaped at his hard, bronzed chest and its fine layer of dark hair. Would he insist she touch it if they became lovers? If so, how would it feel?

No. She would *not* think so . . . immodestly, so shamefully. If her escape were unsuccessful, she would abide by their bargain, but certainly she would not enjoy the man's touch. Nor would she come to his lustful way of thinking.

With that resolution, she turned her attention to his breeches lying on the floor at his feet. A hopeful breath caught in her chest as she searched for a pocket.

Straining not to make a sound, she explored the garment, only to find it had no such pocket. Grabbing a voluminous shirt, she patted the front in search. Her fingers closed around soft fabric—then something small and hard. Victoria fought to restrain her cry of joy.

Noiselessly, she followed the object, finding it was a key tied with a string and tangled in the buttons about the shirt's neck. Elation surging, she snatched up the key and returned his shirt to the floor.

Scurrying across the room, Victoria exited, shutting the door softly behind her. She prayed the sound wouldn't wake him. Barefooted, her heart drumming, her blood pounding, she sprinted to the gate.

Her trembling fingers inserted the key and turned it. Freedom was hers! And she might be hours away before he woke to find her gone. Hopefully by then, she would be halfway to London, back to Dalmont. They would wed soon. Her future would be safe.

Iron fingers wrapped around her wrist and spun her about. There Dominic stood, anger slashing across his dark face.

"Let me go." She writhed for freedom like a mad-woman.

He paused not a moment to consider her plea. "Give me the key, Victoria."

He looked dangerous in the moonlight, his face all angry shadows, his bronzed chest all hard angles and unyielding planes.

Refusing to capitulate, Victoria clutched the key in her white-knuckled grip. If he killed her, at least she'd die trying to win her freedom.

"Give it to me," he repeated.

"Leave me be!"

"I will have revenge, Victoria. We will be lovers. That is the bargain we struck."

Resisting the urge to remind Dominic that taking her to his bed would not bring Marcella back, she stared at the granite green of his eyes. This vendetta drove everything Dominic did. It filled his eating, his sleeping, his breathing, like an insidious infection eating at his soul. Such an obsession could only be born out of deep pain. Or a deep love.

Then the truth struck Victoria. She looked to Dominic, eyes wide with a sudden realization. "You loved Marcella, didn't you?"

Stonily, Dominic glared at her. His look neither confirmed nor denied her theory, but she felt the heat of his instant rage.

"Give me the key," he commanded, a thunderous frown crossing his features.

"I am right," Victoria asserted, holding the key behind her back.

Yet suddenly she prayed her theory was wrong. Had he thought of Marcella while claiming her own lips with the tender vibrancy of his passion? Humiliation hit her.

"You knave!" she lashed out. "I will not let you use me further."

"Give me the bloody key!" he repeated, grabbing for it.

"You love her still." Her whisper sliced her with some unnamed emotion she prayed would vanish. She didn't want to care about Dominic Grayson, his betrayals or his pain.

With the breadth of his sleek-hard body, he pinned her against the wooden fence. His hot glare seared her. In his eyes, she saw pain so deep, so raw, her heart crumbled.

No doubt, he still loved Marcella.

He plucked the key from her hand and locked the gate. "My feelings for my wife are none of your damned business."

Six

Four nights later, Victoria lay awake, despite the fact midnight had just passed. She listened to the soft sounds of Grayson's even breathing, uncertain what to do.

What she had learned of Dominic's feelings for his wife while they fought over the gate key told her so much, yet so little. Yes, she'd seen the anger in his eyes. Yet she had also glimpsed pain, two endless green pools of it. Had Marcella's betrayal with Dalmont caused that gash in his soul, or was it her murder? Was his pain a husband's grief or a killer's remorse?

Victoria had no answers for his behavior—or her own. Despite her suspicions and this abduction, she could not banish the woman's ache he created. She wanted him more with each passing moment. What was it about Grayson that evaporated her logic like water beneath the parching sun?

Half of her believed he was capable of killing his wife in a moment of betrayal's passion, believed in the viable anger that always lurked under the surface of his facade. But the other half doubted the easy judgment. If he were a cruel man by nature, he would have raped her when he'd had the chance. Certainly, he wouldn't care if she felt pleasure in his bed.

She sighed. Was he a depraved killer who hid his evil well or a grieving man driven to retribution?

If the latter, Grayson had certainly given his life, his soul, to avenge Marcella's death, and she could only conclude that he had loved her deeply. Though it defied logic, when Victoria thought of another woman possessing Dominic's heart, an emotion that felt suspiciously like envy tripped through her. What would life be like as his woman and not his captive? To have his affection? To wake beside him each morning, feeling his lips touch hers with a tender kiss?

Marcella must have been a true creature of beauty and wit for a man as fascinating as Dominic to fall so hard for her.

Sighing, Victoria wondered why she tortured herself with such thoughts. Because Dominic was the most beautiful man she had ever seen. Because he kissed her so thoroughly, her toes curled. Because he was an intriguing puzzle, despite the illogical nature of her attraction.

Victoria sat up for a peek at her captor. Dominic lay on his back, eyes closed, resting his palms against the flat planes of his bare abdomen. The smell of brandy and smoke combined with the misty scent of rain and sandalwood. Closing her eyes, she inhaled deeply, finding the odor, so different from any at Wilton House, distinctly pleasing.

"You're still awake?" Dominic sat up on his pallet on the floor, startling her.

Victoria met his eyes warily across the firelit room. "Yes."

"Do you feel unwell?"

Concern registered in his voice, warming a spot in her heart. Knowing it was foolishly dangerous to do otherwise, she pushed that feeling aside. "I feel fine. Just . . . restless."

"A warm brandy might help," he suggested, gesturing to the bottle on the mantle.

"My father never permitted me to drink spirits."

Dominic smiled, his face transforming into a breath-catching dichotomy of masculine angles and boyish mischief. "Your father is not here, my lady. A nip or two won't hurt you."

Looking away, Victoria stared at her folded hands self-consciously. "Are you certain? He always told me I would faint from the drink's strength."

Dominic cleared his throat, stifling a laugh. "Pure rubbish, I promise. Drink some." His whispers reached her, dancing shivers across her skin. "And if you fall, I will catch you."

With that assurance, she stepped to the fireplace and measured out a dose of the liquor. After pouring it in the kettle dangling above the fire, she turned to wait as the liquid warmed and found herself gazing at Dominic, half-hoping she would faint just so she could feel his arms around her again.

He sat mere feet away on the floor, a fist beneath his chin as he directed a seeking green stare at her. The bare skin of his hard chest glistened in the muted gold of the firelight.

Neither said a word. Victoria fidgeted with a handful of her lawn gown. Stomach dancing, palms sweating, self-consciousness assailed her. She listened to the snapping tongues of the flames pervading the room, emphasizing the charged silence. It stretched outward and onward into a chasm Victoria had no idea how to cross.

As if sensing her discomfort, Grayson said, "Tell me of Wilton House."

Relieved to have a familiar topic, she answered, " 'Tis the most beautiful place in England. I used to take my dolls beneath its cherry trees and we'd while away the afternoon taking tea together." She paused, her mouth turning up in wistful remembrance and continued, "Whenever I wanted a moment alone, I would hide in the garden's *al Italiano* pavilions, where I could indulge in my love for drawing for hours."

"You draw?" His voice rose in interest.

"And paint, ever since I can remember," she said with a nod.

"Anything in particular?"

"Sometimes animals and people, but mostly Wilton House. Anything, really. Drawing is my passion."

"So I see."

At his husky tones, she felt her smile fall and began nibbling on her lower lip. He probably thought her addle-brained, indeed. "I didn't mean to prattle."

"Not at all. I enjoy hearing of your . . . passion." His gaze locked with hers, his eyes oh-so-green and challenging. "Your face lights up when you speak of it."

Disquieted by his unwavering stare and soft voice, Victoria turned away. Bringing up passion, any passion, in his presence could only lead his mind—and hers—toward the ultimate passion, something she would never share with him.

Silence ensued again. She heard his soft breathing, the rustle of his sheet. Her mind's eye flashed her a vision of his naked chest, bronzed and powerful. Her belly did flops. As her thoughts wondered back to the forbidden topic of passion, she wondered if his touch excited as his words did. Contemplating that with a sigh, she reached for the kettle.

The handle slipped through her fingers and fell, tipping sideways. Hot liquid rained down, spilling on her hands. Searing pain hit her instantly. She screamed, trembling in horror as she stared at her fingers and the back of her palms, watching angry red blotches form. Fire seeped deep under her skin.

Beside her, Dominic's strong hands suddenly gripped her wrists. "Let me see."

Cursorily, he examined her hands. Victoria glanced at his strong profile, somehow feeling calmer with his assistance, and saw concern in his expression.

"Come with me," he said, leading her out of the cottage, through the darkness, to the pool's edge.

He knelt, tugging on her arm, urging her to kneel beside him before the clear water. Reeling with the sting of her burns, Victoria felt her legs fold beneath her, and her knees land on soft earth. Holding her wrists, Grayson plunged her hands into the clear, cold water. Relief flooded her.

Dominic reached up a soothing hand and stroked her hair. "How does the water feel, my lady?"

The soft magic of his tender, reassuring touch surprised Victoria. She reveled in its soothing effect. "Improved."

Dominic nodded, eyes moving over her face with concern. "Stay here and keep your hands in the water. I'll be back."

Victoria concentrated on the scents of rich earth and dew-dipped grasses until Dominic returned moments later, carrying strips of clean, soft linen, a small vial, and a steaming mug. He set the cloth and the vial aside. "Try some brandy now."

After she nodded hesitantly, Dominic raised the rim of the mug to her lips with a warning. "It is still hot. Be careful not to burn your tongue as well."

Dominic tipped the cup to her mouth. Studying him, Victoria partook of his offering, unable to say nay to the intimacy of his gesture. Again, he'd shown her a new, concerned side, a part of him she had not known existed. What else did he hide deep within?

He cradled the back of her neck as the sweet liquid burned a path from her throat to her stomach. When the cup was empty, he set it aside. The brandy settled in her stomach, and in minutes, her body turned warm and languid; her head felt light, as if she floated on mystical waters.

Soon, Dominic removed her hands from the pond and again studied them in the moonlight. After uncorking the vial, he applied pomatum, then wrapped her hands in the linen.

He leaned close. Sweet heaven, so close she smelled his uniquely musky scent, the body heat he radiated, his soft exhalations as he examined her hands with care.

As if sensing her scrutiny, he lifted his head slowly, slowly, until his gaze found hers.

She swallowed when those green-gold orbs focused on her face, then dropped to her mouth. His eyes darkened. Victoria felt her heartbeat accelerate in response. Her traitorous memory provided vivid images of his salty-sweet kiss. The impact of her remembrances collided with her inner warnings to look away.

"It will hurt tonight, but you'll soon heal."

Even his voice, strained yet filled with relief, sharpened the yearning within her. Had he truly been concerned about *her*? Or was he merely worried about the instrument of his vengeance? His touch, his words, said otherwise. And foolishly or not, she wanted to believe he cared for her as a woman, if only for a moment . . .

She couldn't move, could barely breathe—and continued to stare.

His lips were firm, their set troubled. They seemed to cry out for her touch, yet dare her to close the scant inches between them at once. The provocative curve of his mouth, coupled with her need to feel his comfort, sparked another urge to touch him.

As if he'd read her mind, his hand rose to the sensitive small of her back. His yearning expression, the gentle pressure of his touch, told her he felt the same need as she.

"Victoria," he whispered, his voice raspy, unrecognizable. She didn't know if the word was an endearment or a curse.

The atmosphere between them hung heavy and charged. His fingers tightened at her waist. She tried to tear her gaze away, but the potency, the need, she saw alighting his eyes scorched her into stillness.

He brushed his hands up the length of her back to her shoulders. Tingles leapt to life across her skin. With nothing but moonlight and night sounds around them, his eyes conveyed need and hunger in his dark face. He smelled of brandy and musk and man. His thin white shirt, donned in obvious haste, exposed a section of his smooth, powerful chest. Her stomach fluttered. Would he kiss her? Did he want to?

Dominic's hands cupped her cheeks as he pulled her closer to his rugged face and yearning gaze.

She was lost.

His lips captured hers in a kiss both elemental and imploring, both taking and giving. The warmth in her stomach turned hotter in an instant.

He emitted a raspy breath that became a hoarse

groan as his tongue slipped past her open lips to reap of her mouth.

A current of shock flowed through her at the unexpected touch. The air left her body in a gasp of surprise and passion. She'd never imagined anything so . . . intimate, so arousing. She melted against him, meeting his tongue with her own, and clung to him tightly, clutching his shoulders.

Dominic found the sleeve of her lawn gown. With a brush of his fingers, he pushed it down, exposing her shoulder. His palm slid across the bare skin, teasing the side of her breast. Suddenly, she ached for his touch there, where she had feared it just days ago. Victoria held her breath as his hand slid downward, inching closer. His gaze seared her taut nipples as he bared her breasts completely.

Shaking, Victoria swallowed, wondering what would happen next, knowing she should push him away . . . knowing she was unable to do so. Her gaze traveled to his face, seeking an answer.

He met her stare. The promise of desire fulfilled charged his gaze, singeing her. For the first time, her emotions outweighed her modesty.

Finally, his shaking hand caressed the side of the taut globe. Her flesh responded to his warm fingers immediately, tightening, turning heavy with desire for more.

He slid his mouth down her jaw and kissed the side of her neck, then her collarbone. His nearness and scent surrounded her. In pleasure, she arched, her head falling back, her eyes closing. Her fingers found their way into the waves of his soft, ebony hair, and she clung as his lips descended ever downward.

"Victoria . . ." he whispered.

His mouth closed around her breast. She gasped,

pleasure infusing her. The rosy nub hardened against the silky abrasion of his tongue as he swirled it about, driving her to gasping madness.

Urgent fingers grasped the sides of her waist. His gaze lifted to hers, unutterably hungry and seeking.

"End this maidenly protest now," he whispered against her breast. "We want each other. Share my bed, love."

His words were a dash of icy water on her ardor. Dear Lord, she had nearly allowed her captor, a possible murderer, a man whose heart belonged to another, to touch her. What had she done? Nothing she hadn't ached for him to do. Wondering if she'd lost all sanity, Victoria jerked away, pulled her gown over her shoulder, and covered her breasts again.

"I raise no maidenly protest without good cause. Why do you imagine I will simply lay down for a man who abducted me, much less share such intimacies with one I scarcely know?"

Comprehension swept across his features as he stood tall before her again. "Do you say you want to feel as if you know me, as if we share secrets, before we share my sheets?"

"I—"

"I am eight and twenty," he cut in to her protest. "I have lived in England my entire life. I grew up an orphan in Cornwall after my parents died when I was but six."

"I'm sorry," she whispered, feeling an unwanted pang for a boy who lost his parents as a youth.

He shrugged. "The ladies at the orphanage treated me well. Now that you know of my life, come inside with me."

Victoria's mouth dropped open in incredulity.

"Wouldn't the ladies be proud of you now, abducting innocent women and seducing them into sins of the flesh?"

Gritting his teeth, he said, "Playing on my conscience will change nothing."

"I had no expectation it would. You must be possessed of a conscience first."

"I see you want more information." He cleared his throat before returning to their previous topic. "When I turned eight-and-ten, I received a comfortable inheritance from my parents' estate. I make my home in a country house in Surrey. Is that sufficient?"

His crass suggestion that a few details of his life would encourage her to part with her clothes vexed her . . . along with the realization that he had said nothing of a truly personal nature. Nothing of his feelings, his boyhood ambitions, his dreams, his past.

"When did you meet Marcella?" she asked, testing him.

With her question, a chill descended on the shadowed contours of his chiseled face. "What she and I shared is in the past. Leave it there."

"How dearly I would love to, but you are clearly disinclined to do so. My abduction proves that."

His jaw tensed as he looked away. "My past is none of your affair."

She clenched her fists. Would the man never understand? "When it affects me, it's very much my affair."

"Jealous?" he accused. "You know, sharing my roof and a few kisses gives you no right to all the details of my life."

His hurtful words snaked around her heart, squeezing until it hurt. "Then share your roof and your kisses with another woman, preferably one who's willing. I will happily leave."

Bursting with anger, Victoria turned for the cottage, all but marching to it. Dominic wrapped a tight hand around her elbow and hauled her back to his side.

She snapped her gaze in his direction, showing him the full measure of her fury. He met her stare for a heartbeat, then two, before abruptly releasing her.

"I cannot let you go. You know that," he whispered.

"You won't let me go. There is a difference."

He sent her a silent nod of concession.

"And despite your belief otherwise, I've no intention of sharing your bed. Ever."

His face tightened, the carved planes hard and unreadable. "Why not, my lady? You seemed willing enough a few moments ago."

Fury shot through her body, despite the fact he spoke true. Fighting an urge to rail at him, she pasted on a falsely sweet smile, then kicked his shin.

With a yelp, he grabbed his leg and shot her a glare that promised retribution. "These petty assaults won't change anything. We will be lovers, Victoria."

She cast him a mocking smile. "Clearly, you're not accustomed to having your advances refused. I suggest you learn."

"Do you have any brains amongst you?" Phillip ranted at the dozen or more men who stood inside his town house's parlor.

"Lord Gaphard," he directed to the man at the front of the pack, "make them understand this is my fiancee! She is incapable of defending herself against a ruthless killer. God's Blood, doesn't that warrant your full effort?"

"Your Grace, please, remain calm. I know you fear for Lady Victoria's safe—"

"Of course I do," Phillip spouted. "Surely the reward I have offered is sufficient incentive. Find her, damn it, and return her to me."

"I am doing everything possible to see to that end. My men and I have scoured the ports of London, Dover, Calais, and every small town surrounding each."

"Search them again," Phillip demanded. "And broaden your scope."

"As you wish."

Phillip slammed his fist against the table. "Damn Grayson! He will pay for this. If he has touched her once—"

"You must calm yourself, Your Grace."

"Calm myself? When he may likely bed and beat the woman I'd planned to wed?"

Tight-lipped, Gaphard offered, "I shall double the number of searchers and send them all round the country. We'll question every man, woman and child, if we must."

Phillip nodded. "Once Grayson is found, I want him slain on sight. I want no government interference, no trial where he might be found innocent, and no prison from which he might again escape. I want him dead."

"I understand, Your Grace. Perfectly."

Seven

Dominic stared at Victoria as she lay curled enticingly on one side of his bed, her hands tucked beneath the pillow. As she slept, her eyes drifted open, then half-closed again. At her slumberous, seductive expression, he cursed. Desire surged again, an ache to strip himself of his breeches, tear away her night rail, along with her fears, and bury himself within her tight sheath while hearing her pleasure-filled moans.

He grunted bitterly. And someday, men would fly.

The bite of his edgy mood could only be attributed to the disturbing heat of Victoria's sensuality. Last night, after their kiss, he'd tried to sleep, but found his man-hood too hard, his imagination too vivid . . . and his logic terrifyingly absent.

This morning, nothing had changed.

He had never seen skin like hers, so very fair. Now, knowing exactly how soft that skin was only charged his desire further. Her natural scent, an enticing mixture of soft spring flowers and the mist after a summer rain, lingered in the air.

How would she feel beneath his hands? Naked against his body? He shook the thought away. She was merely Phillip's intended, a pawn in his plans. There was nothing extraordinary about Victoria Tarrent.

Except her bravery.

Her astonishing defiance in the face of her abduction surprised him, along with the occasional, well-placed dig at his plans and motives. Hell, she had even threatened him with his own knife. Hardly the behavior of the quiet, country-bred miss he'd expected.

She personified temptation, and he needed her almost as much as his next breath. He couldn't seem to look his fill or make love to her enough in his mind to drive her from his thoughts.

Disgusted with his lack of self-control, Dominic forced himself to look away.

Forgoing his morning coffee, he left the canyon to hunt, his mind still a tangle of silken arms, ocean-blue eyes, and berry-moist lips. The morning-misty hills and cloudless dawn caught only his passing glance. In fact, he'd scarce had a moment's peace since kissing Victoria. He wanted her, more deeply than he remembered ever wanting any woman. Not a good omen for his objectivity.

The sharp crack of a pistol startled him from his reverie.

Jerking his head to the sound, Dominic made out a band of riders breaking through the trees in the distance. Armed riders, apparently shooting at the morning's game. He frowned. Such a pack of men in this area was uncommon.

A slow sweat formed on his brow as he found an outcropping of rock nearby and hid behind it, just in case Phillip's reach had, indeed, stretched this far.

Dominic glared at the front rider, a bearded brute he'd swear he recognized as Dalmont's chief thug. Crouching lower, he cursed.

The men spread out in several directions, examining

the surroundings. One man, a lanky man on a roan, rode within ten feet of him. His heart pounding, Dominic held his breath and prayed.

"See anything?" the familiar-appearing man asked.

"Just this," the tall sentry answered, scooping up a dead hare.

The leader spit out a curse. "Let's keep moving, gents. We must find Grayson."

After interminable moments of holding his breath, Dominic watched the riders pass. Slowly, he stood and rubbed damp palms on his trembling thighs. Until he'd seen those men, he had not believed Phillip could find him. Now he wondered. And feared, for he could almost feel the shackles around his wrists again, cutting, cold against his bleeding skin.

He would die before going back to the hell of Newgate and suffering Phillip's injustices.

But what of Victoria? Phillip wanted her back, that much was clear. Dalmont desired to bed her; and for the privilege, he would wed her. For reasons Dominic didn't want to examine, the vision of her in Dalmont's arms punched him with a jab of jealousy. He shook it away, wondering about her future. What would happen if Phillip wedded and bedded her? Would he kill her, as he had Marcella, once he tired of her?

The possibility filled Dominic with panic. He had to convince Victoria of the truth, protect her from what she didn't believe in . . . preserve her dreams of love and marital bliss for the man who could fulfill them.

Dominic suppressed a sudden urge to be that man. Not that he loved her—but disillusioning someone with such seeming innocence troubled him. What if she never found a man worthy of her dreams and attentions? Would she die lonely and bitter?

Pushing the thought away, Dominic chastised himself. He couldn't worry about her tomorrows. He wouldn't be a part of them.

With an unsteady gait, Dominic made his way back to the canyon. He must put revenge before Victoria, before his fascination with her sharp mind and pliant body. Plotting ways to thwart Dalmont would be more productive.

Opening the canyon's gate, he navigated his way down the hill, then spied Victoria sitting beside the pond. She'd lifted her dress about her knees to dangle her feet in the chilly water.

An expanse of ankle and calf lay exposed to him. His loins tightened when he espied her face tilted to the watery sun like a goddess in offering to her pagan worshipers. Pale rays illuminated the unbound mass of her cinnamon tresses, turning them fiery red from the top of her head to their ends, where they lay against the ground, teasing her fingertips.

A moment later, a wave of dizziness assailed Dominic. He realized he'd forgotten to breathe.

How could he want her so much? Knowing that she had kissed him willingly, that some part of her was curious to explore their growing attraction, only heightened his desire for her. And not just for her body. He found he wanted to know her mind. Why, he didn't know exactly; but he could not quell the impulse.

Damned dangerous desires.

Just then, she peered at him through eyes squinting against the cheery morning sun. "Why do you stand there, wearing such a fierce expression?"

Clearing his throat, Dominic blustered his way toward her, praying she had no idea how badly he wanted to touch her, how much he was beginning to wish they weren't enemies.

"I'll be traveling today to the nearest village."

The words popped out. As he registered her surprise, he realized it was for the best. This way, he could arrange for Andrew to leave more false clues, stock up on fresh foodstuffs—and try to forget his captivating captive.

"A village?" She frowned. "Isn't that dangerous for you? You could be seen or caught."

Suspicion hardened his features. No matter how sweetly she'd allowed him to kiss her last night, she wasn't likely to forget he was holding her against her will. He'd best not forget it, either.

"Your concern is touching, my lady. But without an organized police force, I'm not in much danger from King George's Charleys. The real threat is your betrothed. You don't know the depravity he is capable of."

She stood, smoothing out her skirts, then put her hands on her hips. "You accuse my betrothed of your crime again and again. Tell me one reason I should believe you."

Dominic hesitated. He was not an impulsive man, but everything within him wanted to tell her all he knew of Phillip Dowling. Undecided, he stared at her bare toes peeking out from beneath her dress, like those of a girl, untouched, innocent.

"See," she accused upon his silence. "You cannot even concoct a reason I should believe in the duke of Dalmont's guilt. Admit your crime."

His patience snapped. For over a year, he'd been treated with scorn, hate, and terror. No more, not from the woman he ached to kiss until neither could breathe, make love to until neither could move.

"Marcella grew to fear Phillip during her six months in his bed."

Dominic watched Victoria's face for a reaction to his words. She returned his stare warily, listening.

"I saw her not long before her murder. Though she tried to hide them, her face bore bruises. She claimed she'd fallen; but she possessed grace, and in the two years of our marriage, she had never taken any such tumble."

Victoria swallowed, her mind racing. Had the woman really suffered at Dalmont's hands? Or was it another of Dominic's ploys to convince her of his innocence so she would abandon her plans to wed his enemy and fall into his bed?

"Marcella acted frightened," he continued. "She claimed she must speak to me later. Shortly after, my maid found her body in my London town house— bloody, bruised, naked, and stiff."

Grayson's face betrayed no emotion in particular, just a tense facade. Was he guilty? Anxious? How could he feel so little for the woman's violent passing?

"If you didn't kill your wife, how did her body come to rest in your home?"

"I don't know."

"Why would Dalmont kill her? What did he stand to gain?"

"Nothing I know of."

"While you stood to gain your freedom from a cuckolding wife," she pointed out.

His mouth thinned into a compressed line. "Yes."

"You were surely angry with her adultery," she prompted.

"Not enough to kill her," he bit out.

Victoria shrugged. "So you say, but certainly her behavior was . . . disagreeable, at the least."

Dominic marched to her in long strides and grabbed
her shoulders. "I did not kill the woman. Yes, she angered me. Yes, I wanted her amorous pursuits with my
best friend to stop. But not enough to end her life with
my fists. Hell, if I had killed her, do you think I would
have left her body in my own home, when I knew the
maid would find her?"

His question took Victoria aback. She could describe
Dominic Grayson in many ways, but illogical was not
among them. Certainly if he had killed Marcella, he
would have taken the body elsewhere to avoid incrimi-
nation. And if Marcella's body were already stiff, the
woman had probably been dead for some hours, plenty
of time for Grayson to have moved the corpse.

Could he possibly be telling the truth?

Pulling from his grasp, Victoria sent him a measuring
stare. "Even Dalmont had no motive. How can you be
certain he killed Marcella?"

"He told me."

As Dominic turned away, Victoria wanted to deny his
words as preposterous. But his explanation had a chilling ring of truth to it she couldn't quite dismiss.

Had Dominic been telling the truth about everything—the murder, her betrothed's true nature—all
along?

When Victoria woke the following morning, she was
alone, though she had heard Dominic return from his
journey deep within the night's hours—after she had
exhausted herself in trying to escape the locked gate.

Stretching sore muscles unused to climbing, she
made her way to the coffee, still warm above the fire.

Dominic's words from the day before rang in her head. She could scarcely believe that Dalmont had told her captor that he'd murdered his wife.

According to Dominic, the duke of Dalmont had covered up his crime by framing Marcella's cuckolded husband and explained away his taunting confession to Dominic as the rantings of a jealous fiend when asked of it by the authorities. Was it possible the duke had framed Dominic for his own wife's murder? She shook her head in confusion. Dalmont had no motive to perpetrate such an elaborate hoax. Still, it seemed unlikely that Grayson would have kept the body in his own house . . .

Pouring the steaming coffee, Victoria noticed two large packages on the battered oak table. Curiously, she approached them, then picked up the small piece of paper which lay on top. *For you,* it read. And though it was not signed, Victoria knew the scrawl could only belong to Dominic.

Victoria tried to tell herself not to care, that he had only bought her something to assuage his conscience. After all, he planned to use her in the most basic way a man could use a woman, and made no attempt to hide that fact.

Maintaining that thought, she opened the first package slowly. But her resolve melted when she saw the contents: Drawing tablets and charcoal!

With haste, she tore into the second package, and was stunned to find the treasures of canvases, paints, and a variety of soft-hair brushes.

She rushed outside in a state of near elation and found him stooped behind the cabin, stacking the firewood he had finished chopping. His shirt lay aside, abandoned for the blue-cool breeze of the spring morn-

ing. His bare back, glistening with sweat, faced her.
Again, she noticed the strength, the bronzed power of
his flesh. A tingle started low in her belly.

Words left her as she watched his shirtless labor. Her
eyes coveted him as her memory relived those muscles
beneath her fingertips after their kiss by the pond. She
could almost feel the wet warmth of his mouth on her
breast . . .

Victoria chided herself for such an immoral weakness. She must remember that he had taken her from
her family and her future, must focus on the debasing
plans he still had plotted for her. Must remember he
might be a murderer.

"What do you want?" he asked before she could turn
away.

"How did you know I was here?"

Finally, he faced her. His face, tanned and flushed
from his exertions and the morning sun, was framed
by raven hair, damp with perspiration at the temples.
His eyes looked intensely green in his golden face as
his gaze met hers. The jolt of their contact registered
in her every nerve.

"I felt it," he answered.

Victoria understood that. She felt his presence
keenly, too, particularly now, when the air between
them seemed thick and charged with something she
had just come to understand was enticing but dangerous.

Dominic raised jet brows in question at her silence.
"I asked what you wanted."

Her eyes dropped to the hard ridges of his chest. No
matter how dastardly his actions, a wicked part of her
yearned to roam the silken steel of his skin, to explore
and experiment. She also felt an inexplicable certainty

that if she gave in to her desire, she could quiet the anger within him that demanded revenge, give him a measure of peace . . . while making her body sing.

Suddenly, he grabbed her arm and backed her against the wall of the cottage. Her lips parted on a gasp of surprise.

"Never mind. I know what you want," he growled. "Heaven help me, for I want it, too."

He slanted his mouth over hers fiercely. His tongue invaded, ravenous, stroking, igniting fire within her. Swept up in the spark bursting to life within her, she clutched him, her palms covering his sweat-slick skin. With one hand he removed the combs from her hair, with the other, he unfastened the buttons of her gown.

"Sweet Jesus, you feel good," Dominic murmured against her lips as his palm cradled her breast, his thumb teasing the sensitive tip.

"Yes," she moaned.

In aching response, she arched toward him, seeking more of the pleasure he gave so effortlessly. Over the linen of her dress, his mouth followed his hand, encompassing her nipple, his tongue teasing the aching point so slowly.

Drifting down, his palm caressed the sensitive plane of her stomach before sliding between her legs to cup the most female part of her. He rubbed her rhythmically, without hurry, his touch teasing one moment, demanding the next. She cried out.

With that, he backed away, his chest rising and falling with deep breaths. "How can you make me want you so quickly, so completely?"

As Victoria regained her senses, she replayed his words in her mind, which seemed so like flattery. Yet the tone more closely resembled a reluctant confession.

Confused, she snatched the front of her gown and covered the wet, aching weight of her breasts and crossed her arms over her chest.

"I came here not to be kissed, but to thank you for the things you gave me."

He turned away with barely a raised brow. "It does not matter if you appreciate them."

Pain crossed her face as she sucked in a breath and turned away. "I will never understand you. Do you kiss me to test your manly appeal?"

Dominic scowled. "That is ludicrous. You know why I kissed you."

Pursing her lips, she frowned, then whispered, "Do I?"

He offered no further explanation, only that flat stare with edges frayed by pain she knew was his alone.

"What a contrary man!" she said. "Your touch is warm and giving. And sometimes . . . you make me believe the man can be thus, too. Then you pull away as if I'm lower than a disease-ridden peasant. Despite the few facts you mentioned the other night, I still know little of the real you."

With a warning glance, he turned away. "You see all that is important."

"I see only what you allow me to see—ruthlessness, arrogance, and indifference."

He shrugged. "Perhaps that's all I am."

"I thought so until you called off your assault, until you remembered how much I love art. Until you tried to ease the ache of missing my parents and the life I had planned." She paused. "During those moments, I saw a different side of you. Is that the real you?"

Closing his eyes, he warned, "Do not pretend I am any sort of wounded hero."

"If not, why did you care enough to give me charcoal and paints?" she pressed him.

He looked away. "You're reading too much into a gesture meant to relieve your boredom."

"If you were selfish, why would you worry after my boredom?"

With a curse, he spun around and grabbed her chin, dragging her closer. "You are a flesh-and-blood tool of revenge, Victoria. Don't try to make me into a saint. I want you on your back, naked and willing. There is nothing emotional in that."

Victoria took in the brutality of his words, even as she felt a puzzling fear emanating from him. "My father has often said that those who protest much hide the truth."

"Your father is a smitten fool, his brain soft from the muck of love."

She ignored his derision. "You're simply a different kind of fool—one so embittered by the past, you cannot see the possibilities of the present."

A moment of hesitation later, he said, "I see no possibilities worth considering but lifting your skirts and completing my revenge."

"And then what? What will you devote your life to? Who will be left to care for you when you feel ill or sad or need to share your feelings? Or will you just become an old man who is more bitter with each passing sunset? I scarce imagine that was your childhood dream."

Dominic swallowed and took a long time in answering. "I need no one."

Frustration and something, something like despair, rolled off of him in waves. And she began to understand. When his love for Marcella had been trampled on, he'd sought refuge in hate, solitude, and revenge.

Yet such misdeeds would never fulfill him, and he knew no way back to light and life.

"You can keep telling yourself you need no one, Dominic, if it eases your mind. But everyone needs someone."

"No more!" he roared. "I've been to that euphoria you call love, enough to know better than to wish for it again. I'd sooner rip my own heart out and spit on it."

She arched her brow. "Clearly you speak true, sir, for that is exactly what you do now."

With those tidy words, she turned her back on her angry captor and walked away.

Damn her and her honest blue eyes, Dominic thought, turning restlessly against his pillow. Victoria's words earlier that afternoon rang in his head. What could become of the rest of his life if he lived through this debacle of an abduction? And could he bear to spend the remainder of his days alone?

No, but not long ago, he'd thought to spend the rest of his days with Marcella. Not in perfect marital bliss. There had been too much arguing for that. He had, at least, thought to fulfill the vow he'd made to God to honor and keep her for the rest of his days. He'd broken that promise, along with the one to love her until death parted them.

Dominic had known for some time that his young French bride had taken a fancy to the unlikely friend he had made of Phillip Dowling, duke of Dalmont, on the Continent as a young man. He had ignored the signs of her restlessness, scarce believing either of them would behave with so little honor. Never in his worst nightmares had he believed Phillip capable of such brutality.

He had been very, very wrong.

His naivete had brought him here, to a world of loneliness and hate. A world where innocent Victoria would pay the price for everyone's sins.

A world with no end in sight, God help him.

In the morning's wee hours, a terrible scream awakened Victoria—deep, primal, anguished. Dominic?

All but flying out of bed, she threw her gaze across the room to him as he lay writhing on the floor. Even with no light but that from the dying fire, she could see a fine sheen of sweat covering his bare chest, his shoulders, the tense lines of his brow. Suddenly, he sat up, eyes open.

"Nooo!" he cried out. "What have you done?"

His question, more like an accusation, startled her.

"Nothing. You startled me," she offered, confused.

He gazed into the fire. "You killed her, and for what?"

"Me?" Of what did he speak? "I killed no one."

"Marcella's crime was against me, and you killed her!" His expression could only be termed a snarl.

Still, he did not face her, and Victoria understood that he continued to sleep.

"Now you prepare to die as well!" he called out again.

Cautiously, Victoria made her way to Dominic and placed a gentle hand upon his shoulder. "Grayson, wake up."

He grabbed her wrist, settling her against his tense, heated body. When Victoria tried to wriggle away, his hold grew stronger.

"Why?" Anguish poured from that single syllable, spoken in a harsh male voice.

Wondering if he dreamed the truth, or his twisted version of it, Victoria tapped him on the shoulder again, this time with more force. "Dominic, please wake!"

When her plea garnered no reaction, she slapped him in the face.

His head snapped back. He shook his head as if to clear it, then settled a fuzzy gaze on her. "What happened?"

This time when she stepped away from the half-naked length of his body, he made no protest. Hugging herself to combat a sudden chill, she shrugged. "You must have been dreaming."

Dominic's eyes slid shut and he heaved a large gulp of air. "God, will it ever end?"

Taking a tremulous step closer, she said, "Would you tell me about it?"

"Tell you of blood and regret and murder? You will never believe me."

"I shall try," she offered.

"You won't." He shook his head. "It's all too fantastic to be believed." Bitter irony tinged his laugh. "Probably why this whole nightmare is slowly driving me mad."

Desolation swept across his face as he made his way to the sofa and sat.

"I know your love for her still haunts you. Now that she is gone—"

"I stopped loving her long ago, and she knew it."

His raspy confession hit Victoria square in the stomach. "Long ago? But your anguish—"

"Guilt." He hung his face in his palms.

"For killing her?"

He lifted his head to glare at her again, then sighed.

"Because I no longer loved her and because I held no title, she turned to Dalmont, then my friend, perhaps for spite. Maybe she genuinely cared for him at the time. I don't know. My pride refused to allow me to beg for her favors, so I stood aside. She left.

"Six months later, I finally had need to go to London and saw her about town with a blackened eye she tried to conceal with rice powder."

"The bruises you spoke of earlier?"

Dominic nodded, but said nothing.

"And you believe they were Dalmont's doing?"

Again he nodded. "Her hands shook as she approached me. She whispered, something I don't think she had ever done in her life. She begged me to meet her later, but refused to talk then because Dalmont stood close behind." He wiped a hand across his damp, tired face. "I refused. Three days later, she was dead."

The hum of shock vibrated through Victoria. Before she could think of anything to say, he continued.

"I could have saved her life, if I hadn't been so proud. She left me for a titled man, and I hated her for it. Seeing her only brought the feelings back. And she would be alive today if I had simply believed she needed me." He sighed, dragging a hand through his hair. "The least I owe her is to avenge her senseless death."

Understanding enveloped Victoria like a mantle. All the pieces of the puzzle fit. Dominic's behavior, his anger, his regret, even his resistance of his own emotions, all made sense now. Marcella had not hurt him half as much as he had hurt himself. And not half as much as the duke of Dalmont had hurt them both. It no longer mattered that Victoria did not know her betrothed's motive for the heinous crime. She realized the kind of man who ordered Dominic dead for seeking his revenge, for knowing the truth about the murder, would be the kind of man to kill others as well. She knew only that she believed Dominic.

At her side, Dominic sighed and turned away. "Go back to bed, Victoria. I told you the tale was too fantastic."

She stayed him with a hand at his shoulder. "I believe you."

His gaze whipped back to her face, locking on her eyes. He all but froze. She wondered if he even breathed.

"You believe me?"

She nodded. "It all makes sense now, except Dalmont's motive. But I wonder if we shall ever understand his kind of violence."

"Truly? You know I did not kill Marcella?" A confused frown furrowed his brow.

Victoria sent him a gentle smile. "I know. A violent man would have raped me, perhaps killed me. You did neither."

His eyes slid shut. "I simply couldn't do that to you."

Sliding her palm over his shoulder to his back, she whispered, "I know."

Suddenly, his arms wound around her and he pulled her into his lap, burying his face in her hair. "Thank you. No one but Andrew has believed me since the accusation."

She inched back until she could look into his eyes. A tumble of words, once ready on her tongue, stilled in the face of his expression. Not merely heated with desire. No longer closed and challenging. This time, she read need, along with a tangle of happiness and confusion. As well as something he felt for her, based on the intensity of his gaze, which seemed filled with both understanding and expectation. And hunger.

His gaze dropped to her mouth. Victoria felt her breathing grow shallow, her lips tingle. He lowered his mouth toward her. *Heaven help me,* she thought, meeting him halfway.

Eight

His mouth came oh-so-slowly closer.

Anticipation mounted as a night breeze swept through, disturbing the sheer folds of her lace-edged linen night dress. As Dominic held her, the air around them vibrated with life, a condition she had attributed in the past to fear. But she was no longer afraid of Dominic.

His hair gleamed an inky black in the room's muted light. The tanned skin of his face emphasized his green-gold eyes. Skin of golden steel covered his broad shoulders. Physically, he was male beauty personified. He was neither charming nor gallant, but compelling, magnetic. Inside, lay a man who wore his cross of guilt beneath the facade he consistently used as a shield from others, from pain.

"Say you want me," he murmured, his gaze delving into her eyes, her soul.

She swallowed nervously. "I . . ."

"Your eyes mirror my desire when I look at you." Victoria opened her mouth to rebut, but he stopped her with a fingertip against her lips. "And your mouth speaks of surrender when we kiss." His whisper slid across her skin, smoother than sin. "Let me feel that surrender again."

Victoria found she wanted nothing more than to surrender, to forget the past and the future. She yearned to live here, the moment now, to revel in each instant of the feelings he evoked in her. Did he want the same?

She cast a measuring glance at him. "So you seek to seduce me into fulfilling my end of our bargain?"

"Damn our bargain! I don't want you in my bed because you feel obligated," he growled, grasping her arms. "I crave the feel of your mouth against mine, of your body against mine."

Face flaming, heartbeat wild, she murmured, "I won't have you touch me in revenge."

"Look at me, into my eyes," he commanded, waiting until she complied. "Don't you see how much I desire you, regardless of Phillip, regardless of revenge."

Victoria found the heat of his gaze scorching, whispering a thousand promises of pure pleasure. Trembling with hope, with disbelief, she looked away.

"Victoria." His hands were again on her shoulders, eyes riveting into hers. "You are the most incredible woman I have ever touched."

A heated blast of shock raced through her, followed by a warmer wave of uncertainty. Could he possibly be telling the truth? Or were his words merely designed to persuade her to climb between his sheets?

The weight of his gaze captured hers and held it hostage. She had only seen that on the occasions he had kissed her. Her mind tried reminding her how dangerous this was, how dangerous he was, but to no avail.

She watched desire move across his face, flash in his eyes. Across the scant inches separating them, she smelled brandy on his breath. A potent mix of apprehension and anticipation flowed through her. Denying her own desire no longer felt possible.

The tips of his fingers caressed her shoulder. His fiery touch skated down her arm, leaving behind a path of shivers. He rested his hot palm at her waist. She knew she should move away, but found his hands at her back—and his mouth a heartbeat from hers.

His warm breath touched her lips, speeding a swell of desire through her. His mouth came closer still. "Let me touch you."

Before she could respond, his lips covered hers, softly giving, coaxing. He pulled her closer, fitting her hips intimately to his, letting her feel the evidence of his need.

He groaned as their mouths melted in a long, velvety union. The kiss seized Victoria's breath. His tongue touched the curve of her lower lip, sending her a shiver of erotic need.

He spread his hands through her hair, coiling the curls about his fingers as he released them from their braid. Tilting her face toward his, he deepened their kiss. She inhaled the tangy heat of his skin, desire rising within her like the heat on a summer day.

His tongue swirled around hers, giving, encouraging, instructing. After only a moment's hesitation, she succumbed to the urge to return his kiss.

"You will never know how often I have wanted to do this," he whispered against her mouth.

Their lips met again with greater urgency. He clutched her night dress, his hot hands sweeping across her back, drawing her close enough to feel every inch of his body. His fervor seeped through the sheer gown, penetrating her skin as surely as if they touched flesh to flesh.

His mouth left hers to nibble and kiss the side of her

neck. His breath touched her skin there, sending a flash of tingles from where they touched, straight down.

Again, his lips feathered across hers once, then again, leaving behind the taste of him, teasing her.

He claimed her mouth again, the impassioned sweep of his tongue spiraling desire within her to delicious heights. He tasted of a disturbing mix of virility, single-minded intent . . . and desperation.

Without breaking the kiss, he rose, lifting her feet from the floor. With a gentle nudge, he urged her to wrap her legs around his hips. Immediately, he lifted a hand to cradle her bottom and nestle her closer.

He carried her to the bed, then followed her to the mattress, half covering her body. His mouth was on hers once more, unrelenting. She met his passionate assault in wonder, succumbing to the roiling sea of sensation inside her.

She felt his throaty groan deep within her, all the way to the place that would eventually accommodate him. Though she fought the dangerous notion, it shocked her with another blast of liquid fire.

With a caress of his hand, her night dress revealed part of her shoulder. His warm breath, the rasp of his tongue against her neck, turned the flames licking through her hotter and higher.

His fingers loosened the tie at her throat, exposing her collarbones and the upper swells of her breasts. He loved the skin he slowly exposed, his fingers breathing over her flesh.

His hand wandered lower, then lower still, finally cupping her breast in his palm. She felt his touch acutely, the soul-searing pressure of his fingers on her sensitive flesh dizzying. Everything within her leapt for him, then yearned for more.

She watched his head move lower. Eyes closing, she swallowed, then cried out when his mouth closed around the hard tip of her breast. The abrasion of the damp fabric against her skin sent pleasure shooting, her back arching. Another low moan slipped from her throat.

"I want nothing between us," he murmured. "I want nothing beneath my hands but your skin."

The blaze within her spread. His shaking fingers pulled the gown from her body, and she felt the sultry night air drift over her bare, fevered flesh.

The green of his eyes flared to new intensity. He stared at her openly, mute wonder in his eyes, desire branding his face. His hand grazed the curve of her waist, then drifted down to the arch of her hip.

"I need you, my lady. Now."

He was all taut, manly muscle—something forbidden and beautiful. And he would be hers if she could find the courage to touch him in return.

"Let your hands guide you," he coaxed.

His words shot tingles across her skin and through her body.

Her once-reluctant fingers were in motion, caressing his shoulders. Victoria moistened her lips, suddenly hungry for the sight of him. His skin had been kissed a gorgeous gold by the sun. The hard structure of his chest and the ridges of his abdomen dared her fingers to explore. She watched the quickening rise and fall of his chest, heard his ragged breathing. And she wanted him.

Slowly, she lifted trembling fingertips to the center of his chest. The heat of his skin scorched her.

His seduction began again, this time with a fervency that shocked her. He whispered erotic suggestions while touching her in places she had never imagined were sensitive. Across her abdomen, along the outside of her thighs, to the backs of her knees, his hands trailed and tingles lingered.

Suddenly, he rolled to his back, bringing her with him so she lay on top. She gasped at the heat of their naked chests meshing together. Her hair spilled around them as he devoured her mouth, reaping her response, leaving her to wonder if his intent was to possess more than her body.

Fueled by curiosity, she continued to touch Dominic in return, beginning with the hard muscles of his shoulders and arms. She felt the angles of his face, admiring the strength and sensuality of his features. She threaded her fingers through his midnight hair, then moved to explore the solid flesh of his torso.

Without warning, he rolled her to her back. He took her wrists in his hands, pinioning them above her head. The expression in his eyes held the primitive emotions churning within him.

His brows drew together intently in question. "Do you want me to stay? To make love to you?"

Shyness washed through her. How did one confess to desiring a man using her for revenge? *Don't think that,* Victoria told herself. He had to want her. The expression in his hazel eyes, the fervency of his words, could not be lies—not tonight.

She swallowed. "Yes."

The word was a mere whisper, but she knew he heard it. Desire whipped across his face, erasing the hesitation that had been there moments ago.

His mouth and hands covered her flesh again, claiming her, heating her blood. From the tender kisses he pressed to the downy skin between her breasts to the thrilling pressure of his hands caressing the insides of her thighs, he gave her no respite, no ease from her spiraling need.

He slid his knee between her legs, parting them. Then he touched the most intimate part of her, lightly at first. That feathery touch sent a shock of heat, of pure sensation, reeling through her core.

With his thumb, he teased the moist flesh above the ever-growing bud of sensation. Victoria heard her own ragged breath, reflecting the clamoring within for something more.

Slowly, he inserted one finger within her unbreached depths. A cry of pleasure rushed up from within her; she bit her lip to keep it inside. He inserted another finger, stroking her inside, building an undeniable heat.

He brought his mouth to hers as his hand continued its intimate invasion. Moistness multiplied where he touched her. She focused on that damp heat, the gnawing ache that felt stronger than she'd believed possible.

His compelling kiss swept through her mouth. His tongue invaded, dancing with hers. His thumb brushed across the turgid peaks of her breast, arousing her until the urgency of her body broke the dam of her resistance.

"Please," she entreated. "Do something.

He lifted his body from her and worked at the fastenings of his breeches. Above her, his sculpted face, half-lit by the moon, registered intensity, need.

"Oh, Victoria." His voice was throaty, raspy. "Dear God, what you do to me . . ."

With a shuddering moan, he moved closer to the juncture of her thighs. Victoria opened to him. An instant later, she felt his tip against her.

Their gazes locked. His eyes, so very green, promised tenderness.

He pressed into her slowly. As he submerged within her, he felt hot and strange. But her body had become a living thing of feverish, fluid arousal, ignited by his innermost touch.

He paused a moment later and swore. Before she could question why, he began easing into her again, a little at a time.

Small stabs of pain assailed her as he probed further within her. She gripped his hand.

Slowly, he pressed deeper, deeper, until he was fully sheathed inside her.

Dominic lay utterly still, perspiration beading at his temples. Again he kissed her, his tongue mating with hers until the tension ebbed from her body. Slowly then, he withdrew, only to fill her again.

Victoria gasped, but experienced little pain. A groan rose from his lips when their mouths met again. His tongue sought hers, tasted of her, demanding she reciprocate.

He wedged a hand between their bodies. The rough surface of his palm cradled her breast. She arched, instinctively thrusting against him.

His hands fell to her hips, fitting underneath, tilting her toward him. He withdrew. Then pressed into her once more. It felt much better this time. In fact, it felt wonderful. Then he repeated the cycle languorously— so very slowly, the ecstasy of it burned through her.

Blindly, his mouth sought hers. His tongue matched the rhythm of his body, entering and withdrawing as he did. Soon she was moving beneath him, wanting something more she could not explain. But he refused to be hurried.

She watched him, taking in his clenched jaw, the rigid control on his face. He, too, experienced the heady searing of his flesh.

Victoria reached for him, her mouth wandering across his, nibbling on his neck. Her hands coasted along the sleek, slick flesh of his back and lower, cupping his tense buttocks, bringing him more fully into her.

A groan rumbled from deep within Dominic, its sound echoing like an arousing chant in her ear. He raised his head and directed a stare to her. The flash of intensity and desire in his eyes speared her with heat.

His pace quickened—withdrawing, entering, withdrawing, entering—until she felt as if her every nerve ending had flocked to the place where their bodies lay joined. Again and again, his fluid strokes propelled her toward an unfathomable explosion she could almost feel.

Dominic filled her, hips grinding, and the peak rushed toward her. She wanted to fight its power, fearing it would engulf her, but his insistent movements pushed her toward the precipice.

Suddenly, her body exploded. She cried out as the spasms streaked through her, leaving her powerless.

Dominic clung to her, tensing. "Oh God, Victoria!" He shuddered, his body rigid, before he collapsed.

A silent minute later, his breathing subsided. Dominic rolled over, bringing her to lie beside him. Drowsily, she laid her head against his chest, enjoying the soft stroke of his hands on her back.

She heard him swallow, then softly call her name. His whisper wrapped around her heart like a comforting hug. She recalled the times she had wished for someone to share her feelings and thoughts, and Dominic felt so like that fantasy man now: tender, warm, and under-standing. She huddled closer in the sanctuary of his arms, the feeling of being cherished blossoming within her.

She slept with a smile.

Slowly, Dominic woke, aware of the rising and falling of soft, female skin beneath his hand.

Not just any female.

Victoria.

He swallowed with the sudden remembrance. Lord, last night had been . . . extraordinary. She had gifted him not only with her innocence, but the treasure of her passion. He remembered the feeling of sinking into her flesh, of drowning in the sensation of her eager, giving response.

Their lovemaking had gone beyond mere physical pleasure. While inside her, he had been able to feel her goodness, touch her soul. She had moved something inside him that felt suspiciously like his heart. Heaven help him.

What had she experienced? Desire, yes; he had felt the proof of that around him, heard it echoing in his ears. But he felt no triumph. The innocent in her had merely responded to his seduction. But the look she had cast him afterward gave him pause.

He saw that expression in his mind, recalled her face glowing with joy, the eyes full of adoration. But it was only temporary, he knew. She would come to her senses soon.

Naturally, she would feel a temporary measure of ten-derness for the man who had taken her maidenhood, if only to satisfy her romantic notions. But he knew the truth: He, a man without title or position, a man stripped of his honor, could never hold her, even if he wanted to risk his heart and future again.

Opening his eyes, he propped his head up. It was a mistake. Immediately, he encountered the sight of her red-gold curls spread wantonly over her pillow. The thin white sheet rode low on her hips, exposing narrow shoulders, full white breasts, and the indentation of her waist above the flaring of her hips.

Heart racing, blood pounding, he contemplated the different, satisfying ways he could awaken her. But he couldn't. She had fulfilled her end of the bargain she would likely consider distasteful this morning. He had promised her he would bed her once and once only.

But when he looked at her, he wanted to make himself a liar and damn the consequences.

Simply justifying last night to his conscience seemed impossible. He had taken from her the one thing he could not replace. Equally disturbing was the knowledge that his selfish desire to make love to her had motivated him, not his urge for revenge. Marcella had not crossed his mind once while he had explored Victoria's body. He had only wanted her one way—hot, wet, and gasping. He had gotten his wish and more.

Dominic rose from the bed. The tormenting emotions of guilt and self-disgust mixed with arousal. With a curse, he paced to the window, scarcely noting the morning flight of chirping birds.

He tried turning his mind to revenge, but her sweet memory refused to be banished. He tried to reason with his desire. She was a forbidden fruit. She represented the type of woman he had never had—most notably a virgin.

But, his body argued, she felt perfect in his arms, in his life. Her presence gifted him with a sense of hope he hadn't felt since before Marcella's murder. Life without revenge, with her by his side, could provide the peace he craved.

Alarmed, he halted his thoughts there. How could he consider abandoning his revenge to wed Phillip's intended? Not that she would consent to wed an accused man who had nothing to offer. Not that he would ever marry again.

But what of the future, when he'd completed his revenge? Clearly, he could not deliver her back to Phillip. He would either use her very ill or end her life for lying with his enemy.

No, he could never give her back to the duke of Dalmont.

Nor could he keep her with him indefinitely.

Dominic paced and cursed, longing for his usual objectivity. He needed perspective, needed to remember Victoria was merely a pawn in the deadly game he and Phillip played. His feelings should be of little consequence.

If she showed any inclination to continue her romantic leanings, he must crush them, push her away if need be. He saw no other method to protect her from Phillip, yet keep her heart free from an unwise entanglement with his own. He could not risk the danger of unchecked emotions running rampant between them. He had to kill any blossoming emotions she might feel, for both their sakes. Now.

Nine

Victoria opened her eyes to find Dominic standing beside the window, his dark hair lying in touchable waves to his nape. He wore tan breeches that fit very well, indeed, and a linen shirt across the hard ridges of his broad chest. Her stomach fluttering in anticipation, she rose.

"Good morning," she greeted him softly, smoothing a self-conscious hand down the night rail she'd donned tiredly during the night.

"Good morning." He spared her a brief glance over his shoulder.

As Dominic turned away once more to stare out the window, he told her without a word that their shared intimacy of the past night had vanished. Had she displeased him somehow?

"Dominic . . . does something trouble you?"

"No," he answered without facing her.

That he spoke false was clear from his tense pose and distant demeanor. Confusion whirled inside her. What troubled him—their lovemaking? A deluge of dread pervaded her.

Certainly, he must know that, after last night, she wanted to share all with him, that she understood love was not certain to be found in an arranged match with a titled man, as she'd always thought. Yet his stance and voice told her he wished her miles away. Still, she felt the burns of his whiskers on her skin, his scent on the sheets wrapped around her.

She wanted to go to him, touch him, ask him to share his thoughts. But she knew this mood, knew without question he would shut her out. He was eons away in his self-made world of anger. Still, something within her urged her to try.

"Will you talk to me?" she asked.

He shrugged. "Of what?

"Last night—"

"Was not the first or last night I have spent with a woman."

Hurt ripped through her, hurt she swallowed to hide. "I see."

"Good," he returned tightly, finally facing her.

She hardly recognized his eyes. Hard and flat, their green depths displayed none of the need from last night. Hurt stabbed her heart. Victoria felt as if he had slapped her.

Of course, she could have tolerated the slight if he had taken her virginity by force. But no, he had stripped it from her gently, seducing her. God help her, she had been only too willing to yield. Hot tears stung her eyes in silent testament to her hurt. Blinking them away, she whirled around, seeking a moment alone.

Dominic swore. In three long strides, he was across the room, blocking her escape with a hand upon the door.

"Where do you plan to go dressed in a night rail?" he asked, his breath warm against her temple.

"It is none of your affair," she spat.

"Wrong, my lady." He grasped her arm, then spun

her about to face him. "I won't have you outside catching your death over a few tears."

"A few tears?" Fury at his callousness, at *him*, enraged her. She threw her head back with bravado. "How can you suggest I would shed tears over you? That you used me more cheaply than a whore is of little consequence."

He grabbed her chin and held it tightly. His hard expression reflected disbelief. Victoria returned it with a defiant stare.

"I did not use you in that manner, Victoria. Never think I did."

His low, controlled denial only inflamed her. "If I do, what harm can you do me? None. So from now on, I shall do as I please. You've stolen what you sought and have nothing with which to threaten me."

She reached for the door's latch. He stopped her, covering her hand with his own.

"That is where you are wrong. I could drag you back to that bed and, at the snap of a finger, think of a dozen different ways to take you, not all pleasant."

Hurt and anger filled her heart in equal measures until the roiling icy-boil consumed her. Victoria curled her fists in self-rebuke. What did she care? Dominic had proved this morning he was indeed a cruel, foul-tempered brute. Last night had been nothing more than a ploy—one she couldn't fall for again.

"I believe you could, you selfish, lying snake. You will never touch me again. I hate you!"

At that, the anger seemed to leave him, and an emotionless cloak took its place. "Then things are as they should be."

Dominic prowled about the canyon looking for something to hit. Irony was cruel, indeed, to take him to the

heights of heaven last night, only to force him to create
his own hell the next morning.

He cursed, striding for the gate. He needed air not
tinged with Victoria's scent, needed space well away
from her and the hurt in her wide eyes.

Needed to forget how perfect she'd felt in his arms.

Tugging at the key dangling from the string about
his neck, he moved to unlock the door. Instead, he
found a piece of paper just under it. Snatching the bit
of paper from the ground, he quickly unfolded it.

> *Dominic,*
> *I bribed one of Gaphard's men for information. He in-*
> *forms me they saw smoke from a chimney one night in*
> *your area, but could not find its source. They are suspi-*
> *cious and intend to give the area a more thorough search.*
> *I will attempt to leave more false clues to deter them.*
> *Corinne's nephew delivered this note. The boy can be*
> *trusted. I will be there soon with more information. Cau-*
> *tion, my friend.*
>
> *Andrew*

Crumpling the note in his fist, Dominic swore
soundly. A cold sweat broke out across his skin, part
fear, part anxiety. Would nothing go right? He had dif-
ficulty enough in dealing with his defiant beauty of a
captive, enough problems subduing his desire for
her . . . and now found Phillip closing in on them,
ready to take Victoria from his grasp!

Dominic feared that all too soon Fate would force
him to choose between a woman who might quickly
grind his heart into shattered pieces or his revenge
against a man who might well kill them both.

* * *

Victoria wandered about the cottage, wishing she could go back in time. If she could undo just one day in her life, she would choose last night. But she had learned from her mistake. As she'd vowed to Dominic, he would never find himself welcome in her bed again.

Minutes later, he entered the cottage behind her and yanked out a small trunk beneath the room's lone bed. With urgent tugs, he rummaged through his belongings. Anything black, he removed.

"What are you doing?" she asked, puzzled.

For a moment, he said nothing. Instead, he found ways to tack or tie the black garments across the two small windows until the cottage was concealed in deep shadows. Then he doused the fire smoldering in the hearth.

"Making certain outsiders cannot detect our presence."

She cast him a confused glare. "Who do you imagine will find us here, where even God has likely forgotten us?"

Raising his hand, Dominic touted a piece of wrinkled parchment. The eyes he turned on her were harsh and desolate. "This says your fiancé suspects you are somewhere near and he intends to free you from me."

She sent him a shrug of feigned indifference, even as fear and hope clawed at her. "I doubt he could please me less."

"Phillip shall have to pry you from my cold, dead hands if he thinks to whisk you back to London with him." The determination in his countenance took her aback. "For over a year I thought of nothing but revenge. I planned carefully to get you under my roof, and here you will stay until *I* am prepared to release you."

"Why keep me at all? You stole what you were seeking last night."

"You're wrong," he contradicted softly. "Every day you are missing eats at his soul."

"But at the end of six months, when I am free, what will become of me, now that I am ruined?"

He gave her a grudging nod. "We will deal with that later. For now, do not forget you're my captive."

She shot him a look of pure hate. "Dominic, you've made it impossible for me to ever forget again."

Knowing sleep would be elusive again tonight, Dominic stared at the ceiling through the muted firelight. His sleeplessness had little to do with the discomfort of the floor. Duty and desire clashed within him constantly, the talons of turmoil never releasing him into the shelter of peace.

Four nights ago he and Victoria had made love. He had not spoken a single word to her since their last argument, and the hurt in her eyes spoke volumes about what was in her heart.

That silence tested every ounce of his self-control. Twenty times a day he reached out to comfort her, to confess his facade. Each time he walked away. His ambivalence scared the hell out of him. She should be the last person on his mind. He had no love to give, least of all to Phillip's intended.

But she remained in his thoughts. The taste of her skin lingered in his memory, along with the sight of her eyes so filled with ecstasy and joy. The candor of her response still astounded him, not just with her capacity for sensuality, but with the breadth of her intelligence, bravery, and trust—along with her desire, which he must extinguish to succeed in keeping his distance.

And at the end of six months, Dominic vowed he would find a haven for Victoria, somewhere to hide until Phillip's anger was somehow contained. He could not bear Dalmont doing her harm. Hell, he could not bear the thought of Dalmont touching her in any way.

He pressed his fingertips to his aching temples, determined to find sleep—until Victoria's jagged, nearly silent cry reached his ears.

Swallowing a lump of guilt, he told himself she was better off without a blackguard like him.

She climbed listlessly from the bed. Unable to deny his concern, Dominic rose from his pallet and faced her.

Their gazes clashed across the room. Angrily, she averted her face and swiped at the tears falling from her red-rimmed eyes.

The place where his heart had once been twisted painfully. As if his feet had their own mind, he crossed the room until they stood a breath apart. Turning her to face him, he caressed her cheek, brushing the fresh tears away.

"No tears," he whispered.

"Don't touch me!" she hissed, pulling back.

He grasped her other arm, holding her close.

"Certainly you heard me." She thrashed against him. "Or have you gone deaf as well as mute? Don't touch me!"

He held fast to her. "My lady, please stop."

With a pose of wounded defiance, she turned her gaze away.

"What can I say to stop your tears?" he asked.

"It's hardly your concern."

"While beneath my roof, everything about you is my concern," he refuted.

"My tears have nothing to do with you," she lied. "I simply long to go home."

His soft sigh was warm on her cheek. "I know you feel neglected."

Something in her belly stirred at their close contact. She thrashed away from him, refusing to admit any truth to his words. "You arrogant knave, I said nothing of the sort."

"You had no need to. I understand."

She should call herself nothing but gullible. Against all reason, she had hoped they would grow closer, that he would come to love her as she had always dreamed someone would. She'd hoped he would hold her through the summer nights to come. Yet he showed no such inclination.

"You understand nothing but your own wishes. State what you want or leave me be," she shouted, turning away.

He gripped her arm again, spinning her to face him. "I think I should say the same."

"I want only for you to remove your filthy hand."

He released her slowly, his gaze focused on her with single-minded intent. "Are you certain you want nothing more?"

"What else could I want from my captor, except perhaps freedom?" she asked acidly.

Dominic shook his head, his face a complex puzzle of emotions she couldn't decipher. "Well then, our parting should be simple and unemotional."

As he turned away, Victoria watched, wanting to deny the hurt and anger that filled her. Their parting? She could still feel the heat of his kiss and recall the tenderness of his touch, and he was already dwelling on their good-bye. How could something so fulfilling mean so little to him? Every night in her mind, he made tender love to her again. His only thought was of when he could be rid of his unwanted captive.

That was fine, she decided angrily. She could stop wanting him, too. And she would escape, soon.

Ten

When Victoria rose the next morning, she expected to see Dominic, taciturn as always, hovering about the cottage. Surprise flooded her when Andrew entered the dwelling, backlit by fresh spring sun. He greeted her with a smile as he rushed to her side. Dominic hovered in the portal, watching.

"As always, your beauty is so deep it wounds, my lady." Andrew took her hand between his. "How have you fared?"

She felt color staining her cheeks at his unabashed comment. "Well enough, Andrew. And you?"

"Dare I hope you thought of me in past days?"

She found his grin contagious. "Perhaps once or twice."

"In that case, I have fared well, indeed," he murmured over her hand before kissing it. "Had you not thought of me at all, I should have had to learn to juggle or walk across water to earn your remembrance."

Victoria laughed, and Andrew drew a light arm around her shoulder. How fun he seemed, glib in the least serious of ways. She had had none of that these past weeks and craved a carefree moment.

She smiled back. "I should enjoy seeing you juggle,

I think. Walking across water, however, will likely earn
you little more than a dousing."

"For you, my lady, a dousing would be well worth
your smile."

Her lips lifted in another grin. A silly retort sat on
the tip of her tongue—until she caught a glimpse of
Dominic.

The tense look on his face intrigued her. Why should
anything she said or did matter to him? After all, he
had all but ignored her since availing himself of her
body.

Clearing her throat, she smiled at Andrew again, determined she owed Dominic no obligation to behave
as he saw fit. She sidled up to Andrew and threaded
her arm through his.

"Have you come all this way to see me, then?" she
asked.

He leaned to her ear and murmured, "Of course,
but we'll let Dominic believe I've come to speak with
him."

"You are wicked, sir."

Andrew's grin was nothing short of naughty.
"Hmmm. You have no idea how wicked."

A sly glance at Dominic proved his ire still rising, if
red cheeks and blazing eyes proved any indication. Victoria forced a throaty laugh. "I'm sure not."

"Enough." Dominic stepped between them, glaring
at Victoria. "Andrew and I have much to discuss.
Alone."

Irritation prickled Victoria at his high-handedness, irritation she vowed to give back in equal measure.

She shot Andrew a charming smile. "Until later?

"I shall count the moments, my lady."

With a pointed stare in her direction, Dominic

grabbed her arm and led her outside. Victoria merely smiled pleasantly at her captor in return. Dominic must learn he wouldn't always win his way, and before she could make good her escape, she was of a mind to teach him.

"Do you have news, Andrew?" Dominic demanded once Victoria slipped from his view.

He would not think about Victoria's flirtations, her smiles to his friend, the invitation in her voice. Revenge, his hate for Phillip Dowling. Yes, those were suitable topics to occupy his mind. His feelings for her consisted only of powerful lust and irritation. He would forget her, eventually.

"Indeed," Andrew answered. "I left more false clues, but I fear Dalmont is catching on. He no longer believes anyone who claims to have caught a glimpse of you. I doubt he will rest until he sees you himself."

"He can wait," Dominic said, "until I am ready to confront him."

"I think not," Andrew contradicted. "As we speak, he organizes a search party to patrol this area in depth. If you leave now and lead them elsewhere, Dalmont might be willing to call off his dogs. But you must do something to lead them astray. If not, it will be a matter of mere days before they find you."

"When do they leave?" Dominic asked, trying to remain calm.

"Within the week. They await only adequate supplies."

"Sooner than I'd thought." With a frustrated sigh, Dominic continued. "Damn. You're right. I must do something. I have planned too long to let revenge slip through my fingers."

He paced away from Andrew, deep in thought. Over and over, he considered a solution to his dilemma. He could think of only one, and every instinct within him rebelled. Logic smothered the sentiment by reminding him of revenge. Even if Victoria had been his heaven and earth while in his arms, she was still his enemy's betrothed.

With reluctance Dominic said, "Tomorrow, I shall leave to spread more false clues. Will you stay here and protect Victoria in case Phillip should find her?"

"Of course." Andrew nodded.

He paused. "See that you leave her untouched."

The verbal gauntlet was nothing short of a threat. Dominic couldn't seem to stop himself from throwing it. The sharp lift of Andrew's tawny brows proved his friend recognized the warning. For a silent instant, the two men remained mute, the moment suspended.

"Have *you* left her untouched, my friend?"

Dominic stiffened. "That was not my plan."

"Even so, if the girl chooses to experience genuine passion after being raped for revenge, I should hardly blame her. Nor should you."

"I never hurt her," Dominic barked.

"But you did bed her for revenge, did you not?"

"I will discuss this no further."

Curiosity dominated Andrew's face. "Is she still a virgin?"

Dominic felt his eyes narrow with his ire. "That is none of your affair."

Finally, Andrew answered, "Perhaps not, but neither is any association I have with her your affair."

Unable to deny the truth of Andrew's assertion, Dominic turned away. If Victoria wanted him, Andrew would bed her. And after the way he himself had treated her, Dominic would hardly be surprised if she strayed to Andrew for comfort—or spite. His fingers curled into fists.

He wanted to warn Victoria of Andrew's lustiness, didn't want to see her entangled with anyone as destined to use and discard her as Andrew. Yet if he did warn her, he'd reveal himself for the jealous fool he was.

God help him. He had no way to emerge unscathed in this ugly situation. He fought against the festering pain in his chest.

"Leave her be." Dominic forced himself to face Andrew again and unclench his teeth.

Andrew shrugged, but Dominic knew the subject was far from over in his friend's mind.

Nor was it over in his own.

With a sigh, Andrew offered, "Dominic, let's not argue. I came here as a friend, not to make you an enemy."

"Then do not betray me as Phillip did."

The words were out before he could stop them. Dominic wondered what possessed him to speak such jealous sentiments.

Andrew frowned, his confusion evident. "Marcella was your *wife*, the woman with whom you took vows. Victoria is no more than your captive, a woman you intended to rape."

Dominic scrambled for a reply. "But her trials these past weeks have been difficult. She has no need to add your seduction and abandonment to her list. And what if she should conceive? Do you imagine an earl's daughter would wed a former servant?"

"Not any more than I imagine an earl's daughter would wed a man accused of murder, my friend."

Andrew's challenging expression and insinuation brought Dominic back to reality. "On that we agree."

"But if she conceives by you? You would not abandon your own child, I think."

Holding in a sigh, Dominic silently acknowledged that truth. It underscored the reason he'd been glad to learn Victoria had begun her menses after their night together. And the reason he should not tempt fate and take her to his bed again.

"There will be no child, Andrew, not by me. Nor will she miss babes before she can safely wed. She has family aplenty."

Andrew looked away. "She did. That is the other reason I've come."

Victoria gaped at Andrew, the impact of shock coiling around her emotions. "No. That cannot be true!"

Andrew touched her shoulder in a gesture of comfort. "I fear it is, my lady. I'm sorry to bring you such ill tidings."

"Surely, my mother is at home with my father."

"She was lost in the fire, my lady. The same fire that overtook Wilton House."

Victoria turned to Dominic, eyes wild, fighting Andrew's words. "Tell me this is all false!"

"I wish I could, Victoria" he said softly, cupping her cheek with his palm.

She felt the sting of tears behind her eyes. "No!" Her eyes welled with more moisture even as her fists beat half-heartedly at Dominic's chest. "My mother and my home! How will I bear such loss?"

"You are strong," Dominic whispered. "And I shall help you."

Victoria's gaze snapped up to his in surprise. His

grave expression held nothing but sympathy and sincerity.

She backed away, not trusting the softness there after days of cold silence. "You?"

Dominic slipped his hand around her wrist and eased her against his chest. "I am not without compassion."

Their eyes clashed for an instant.

"I do not need your pity," she shouted, even as tears fell down her cheeks.

Andrew whispered his sympathy while Dominic reached for her, stroking her hair, soothing her with an intimate whisper and the gentle touch of his hands against her neck, her back.

A distant realization that she shouldn't allow Dominic such familiarity after the way he'd treated her teased at her mind. But the comfort of his strong, sheltering embrace felt so good. She succumbed to her shock and grief and melted against the solace of his warm chest.

Suddenly Dominic whispered, "Hold near your heart the time you had with your mother, the times you spent in Wilton House. You can keep them alive in your memory." He pulled back a fraction to gaze into her face. "I will help you."

The fact he had shared such soft words made her body shake harder with sobs. Through the cloudy vision of her tears, she saw the infinite gentleness in his expression.

"Why?" she asked. "What started this fire?"

"A kitchen fire," Andrew put in. "I hear she tried to help and sent all others away."

"Where was my father?"

"With Dalmont, helping to organize another search party."

Victoria balled her fists. "She was sweet-tempered to a fault and deserved none of this."

"I know." Dominic stroked her hair.

She wrenched away from his embrace, only to pound a fist on the door.

Dominic pulled her away. "I know you're angry. I understand."

"Do you?" She looked into his eyes, shocked to find genuine empathy.

What secrets did he hide that made his understanding possible?

He nodded. "I've lost everyone dear to me, Victoria. Everyone."

Dominic sat in the rocker, holding Victoria in his lap. Though it had taken him nearly an hour, he had finally soothed Victoria into an exhausted wine-induced slumber.

He ran his fingers absently through her copper curls, contemplating her anguish, when he felt a heavy gaze upon him.

When he looked up, Andrew's measuring stare surprised him. With Victoria's needy tears, he'd nearly forgotten his friend. But Andrew's expression told Dominic his friend had been studying his interaction with Victoria.

Slowly, Andrew spoke. "When last I was here, you warned me of developing sentiments for Victoria. Now I wonder if your words were designed to save me or ensure that I kept my distance. After all, I, too, was willing to help her overcome her sorrow."

Dominic's mind flashed an image of Victoria in Andrew's arms, seeking his comfort. Jealousy, tight and inexorable, coiled within him. Unconsciously, he curled his hands into fists. "That's not necessary."

"Why?" Andrew arched a blond brow.

"As you can see, she is calm now."

Andrew scowled. "You did bed her, didn't you? And you want her still."

"That's none of your bloody business." Dominic's voice whipped through the tense air between them.

"It is when your lust is making you illogical. Or is it your emotions, my friend?"

Dominic glared at Andrew, fury racing through his veins. God, how he wanted to say something, anything to refute those comments. But he feared Andrew was right, and any rebuttal he made would be a lie.

Victoria awakened to lingering firelight and the feel of Dominic, warm and bare-chested, by her side. Her head throbbed, from the alcohol she had consumed and the tears she had spent.

She could hardly fathom that her mother and childhood home were no more, lost to the hot violence of a fire. Where would her poor father live? How would he cope without his beloved wife? How she yearned to be with him so they might share their time of grief. But she was bound here by the velvet chains of Dominic's captivity.

She recalled his vow that she would not face her mourning alone and the accompanying heartfelt expression. Why would he make such a promise? Hoping that he cared for her was the dangerous wishing of a lovesick fool. He pitied her, nothing more. She must read no other meaning into his words.

"Victoria?" Dominic whispered.

Slowly she rolled to her side to face him, the straw mattress crinkling intimately. "Yes."

"I'd hoped you would sleep through the night." His voice held concern even while his hand stroked her hair tenderly. "How do you feel?"

It means nothing, she reminded herself sternly. Pulling away from his touch, she answered, "I've a slight headache."

His hazel eyes were so different . . . so gentle, as they had been the night they'd made love. She wanted to melt into his arms and let the hurt disappear with the magic of his touch, but she refused to accept pity, especially his.

"What—of grief or sorrow?" he asked.

She nodded. "Both."

"Were you close to your mother, then?"

"We had our disagreements, but my mother was a good and kind woman. All who met her loved her. She had a quiet way of giving comf—ort." Tears broke into her speech. "I will m—miss her."

As Victoria buried her damp cheeks in her hands, Dominic stroked her head, his palm conveying both gentleness and sadness in his touch. "I remember my own mother so little, except that she smiled a great deal and smelled something of roses."

Victoria looked away, a needle of sorrow for him piercing her. "I'm sorry. Remembering so little must cause you regret."

Dominic raised on his elbow and leaned over her. He sighed, a furrow of pain settling across his brow. "At times. I found the years of my youth most difficult. Then, I often wished my parents near for guidance and comfort."

Her eyes watered at his loss. "I imagine you felt as if you'd lost a bit of yourself."

He frowned, his troubled eyes revealing the naked pain in his soul. "Some moments felt much like that and they angered me."

That explained his understanding of her anger. He had felt the same guilty fury as she. Such empathy from her fierce captor cast yet another softer light on him. How could one man consist of so many complex facets? Yet she felt as if she had begun to understand him.

"I'm sorry," she whispered.

He shrugged. "I am a grown man now and can accept Fate."

Victoria pondered the emotions swirling within her. "I'm not certain I will ever accept such a terrible fate for one so dear."

"Someday, my lady," he whispered. "Someday, you will, though not easily."

"How? I am angry, indeed, I could not tell her how dear she was to me one last time." She covered her aching, tear-swollen eyes with her hands. "I know I have no right to feel that way. She didn't ask to die."

"The anger will fade," he assured her with a gentle caress of her cheek. "What will your father do now?"

"I've no notion," she answered. "Perhaps stay with his cousin Henry in Yorkshire. I could find out if you would but let me—"

"No."

"—send him a letter."

"No." He sighed. "Victoria, I cannot take that risk. If he believes Phillip a fine man, he will share your letter with your betrothed."

"I will reveal nothing of our whereabouts—"

"I'm sorry." Dominic stroked her shoulder. "Truly, I am."

Seething with resentment, Victoria rolled away, turning her back to him. He would always care for his revenge before her, and she must never forget that.

Eleven

At the knock upon the cabin door, Victoria bade Andrew enter, wishing Dominic would come through that portal instead. He'd left her side four long weeks ago, during which she had waited, worried, and prayed for his safe return. She had also longed for him with every beat of her heart.

"Good morning, my lady. What are you painting?" he asked.

"Home."

"Wilton House?"

Victoria sent him a melancholy smile. "Have you ever been to Wiltshire?"

"No, but if all its women are as beautiful as you, I shall venture there soon."

She cleared her throat, finding herself more ill at ease each day with his flattery. "Where are you from?"

He hesitated. "I was born in Paris."

"Paris? How exciting." The city sounded so sophisticated.

Andrew laughed derisively. "My mother was a dancer in a gaming hall. We moved to London after she married a nob's butler."

"Were you raised in London, then, at this . . . gentleman's house?" Victoria asked.

"Gentleman?" he sneered. "Wealth and position do not always make one a gentleman, I discovered."

"When did you leave there?"

"Not long ago."

Victoria stared at him in puzzlement. "Why did you leave?"

A tight smile formed on his thin mouth. "It was time."

Victoria wondered at his oblique response, but said nothing.

Silence lapsed between them. Her mind circled back to forbidden thoughts of Dominic. No matter how hard she tried to convince herself she did not care what happened to him during his absence, she never succeeded.

"What are you thinking?" Andrew asked.

His words forced Victoria out of her reverie. "Nothing of consequence."

"You are a poor liar, my lady." He cast her a reproachful glance. "Now, what's floating around in that pretty head of yours?"

Victoria looked to him in uncertainty, chewing her bottom lip. "Dominic said he would be gone no more than two weeks. It has been nearly four.

A flash of annoyance crossed Andrew's face. "Dominic is one of the craftiest people I know. For months, he was able to sneak into your betrothed's town house at night, despite the fact Dalmont usually posted a dozen watchmen."

"But Dominic was unable to escape prison without your assistance," she insisted, panic surfacing.

"Only because they kept him chained and beat him regularly."

Victoria shuddered. The brutality Dominic had suffered, the injustice which had caused the atrocity to begin with . . . thinking of it never ceased to jolt her every nerve with horror, despite her anger with him.

Seeing her reaction, Andrew reassured her. "Dominic can look after himself."

"Under normal circumstances, perhaps so. But he has a pack of men chasing him. What if he's been caught?"

"Then I shall do something to save him." Andrew paused, then warned, "I say this respectfully, but you should not waste your concern on a man who will never admit any feeling for you."

Victoria flinched at that cold, stark truth. "I know," she admitted, then posed the question burning in her mind for weeks. "Andrew, did you ever meet Marcella?"

His eyes widened. "Dominic told you of her?"

Victoria heard the shock in his voice, saw it in his gray eyes. "A bit."

"I met her," he said finally. "What did Dominic tell you?"

"He said she left their marriage for my betrothed."

"Yes."

"It upset him."

"Upset?" Andrew returned, clearly amused by her understatement. "Infuriated. Dominic even called Dalmont out immediately after their affair began. They were to meet with dueling pistols at dawn. Instead, Dalmont took Marcella to Athens for a month."

Victoria gasped. "Why?"

"Who can say?" Andrew said with a shrug. "Personally, I think Dalmont knew Dominic would kill him. Easily."

Victoria swallowed, trying to force down her despair. Dominic had cared for Marcella enough to fight for her. Since Dalmont had refused to meet justice on the dueling field, Dominic had chosen to mete it out with revenge, using his enemy's betrothed.

As she placed a trembling hand over her mouth, Victoria's mind raced. Contrary to his words, Dominic must have carried feelings for Marcella. Perhaps he still did. Anger and shame at her own naivete bubbled to the surface.

She spun away, fists clenched. "To Hades with him for saying he no longer loved his wife!"

"I don't think he does," Andrew called from behind.

Whirling to face him again, she demanded, "What are you saying?"

"I think he stopped caring for Marcella long before she left. He merely challenged Dalmont to a duel to preserve his honor. Never once did he ask for his wife's return."

A smile lit her face as hope welled within her. Maybe if—

"Yet I doubt he would ever willingly give of his heart again," Andrew added.

Victoria looked to him anxiously. "Was Marcella as lovely as all that?"

"Not nearly as lovely as you, my lady." Andrew reached for her hand and brought it to his lips. "Your loveliness surpasses any I have seen."

She gently withdrew from his grasp, wondering why he persisted with such compliments. "What—what did she look like?"

He hesitated, peering off into the distance as if remembering. "She had dark hair, thick and long, and sultry blue eyes. Her fair skin held the tone of a ripe peach. She was more . . . exotic than beautiful."

Victoria's heart twisted. Perhaps Dominic had, indeed, had a difficult time forgetting such beauty.

Andrew's gaze slid over her, his expression calling her every kind of a fool. "Why all this interest in Dominic's romantic past? When I was here last, you wanted only to escape him."

Her face flushed hot. She turned away to hide the revealing reaction.

"I'm simply curious," she lied. Certainly she couldn't tell Andrew she hungered for more knowledge of Dominic, thirsted to understand why he cared so little for her. Maybe then she could cure herself of this curious ache in her heart.

Andrew frowned. "Come now, my lady. Tell me the truth."

She fidgeted, twisting her hands. "Well, from what Dominic said, Marcella is the reason he sought this revenge."

"In part, but I believe his hatred of Dalmont motivated him more than his love for his wife, if you must know. But if you hope he will come to love you and declare himself, your desire is futile."

Victoria swallowed away a lump of pain, knowing she had certainly lost Dominic, though he had never been hers to lose.

"Excuse me," she whispered, turning away so Andrew could not witness the tears springing to her eyes.

He grabbed her arm. "Don't run."

Her auburn hair swirled in her face, mingling with the sudden tears. Andrew brushed them aside.

"Let me go!" She tried to free her arm, but he held fast.

"Hush, my lady. Why are you crying?"

"You wouldn't understand. I'm not at all certain I do."

Something strange, almost resembling jealousy, skidded across his bearded face. "Unfortunately, I do, all too well. Victoria, you knew Dominic sought to use you in the basest of ways. Did you really think he would love you?"

She shut her eyes, wishing she could also shut out the painful truth of his words. "Two months ago I didn't want to be with him, not even for ten minutes. But since then, I've come to know him, and now . . ." She clutched the sleeve of his shirt. "Now, I want to be with him more than anything. I know it's foolish. He will never return my sentiments."

At first, Andrew said nothing. Across the heavy silence, he raised his fingers to stroke her cheek. "If Dominic did love you, he would never admit it, not even to himself, I fear."

Phillip ceased pacing in mid-stride to address Lord Gaphard. "Have you seen Dominic Grayson again?"

"No. It's as if he has disappeared."

"God's blood!" Phillip resumed pacing. He turned back to Gaphard. "Where did you last see him?"

"In Dover."

Suspicion plagued his mind. "Was he careful to conceal himself? Was he trying to be inconspicuous?"

After a moment's pause, Gaphard said, "He was not out in the open . . . but neither was he completely hidden."

Phillip drummed impatient fingertips against a baroque-style mahogany table. "It's too convenient to be anything but a ruse."

"Perhaps."

"No. Of this, I am certain. I know his mind enough to realize he does nothing arbitrarily."

As you say," Gaphard answered. "I defer to your experience."

Phillip nodded. "I'm going to keep the men in the South. Grayson's hideaway is there somewhere and he wouldn't show himself unless we were too close."

Phillip poured wine for Gaphard and himself. "Are you preparing to ride south yourself?"

"I can, Your Grace. Within the hour, if you'd like."

Phillip sighed. "I cannot sit here idly while Grayson wreaks his treachery on my unwitting fiancee. I will ride along."

Three taps resounded against the town house's kitchen window, startling Corinne. She rushed to the back door and opened it a crack.

She glimpsed nothing in the semi-darkness. Utter silence reigned.

She glanced about the moonlit kitchen, tensing when she saw a dark shadow. She opened her mouth to scream.

An instant later, Dominic appeared, stepping into the silver rays. Quickly, he entered the warm haven, the smell of fresh bread and rosemary tickling his senses, then closed the door behind him without a sound.

"Where are Phillip's thugs?"

"Looking for ye," she whispered. "Now that ye've got Lady Victoria, he sees no need to keep them 'ere."

Dominic nodded, storing that fact to memory. "Where can we talk?"

Corinne looked toward her bedroom, then decided against it. "Outside."

Dominic allowed Corinne to lead him to the adjoining door. The pair made their way through the crisp night air to the manicured garden, finding solitude within cultivated ferns and climbing ivy. Leaves rustled on the crisp wind.

"Is there any news?" Dominic asked.

She slid her arms around his neck. "Always so serious, Nicky. Where's me kiss?"

Dominic brushed his lips against her warm cheek, then grasped her wrists and removed her arms from about him.

When Corinne peered at him suspiciously, Dominic remarked, "I have no time for greetings now. I must hear what you know."

Corinne sighed unhappily, then said, "Dalmont's culls spotted ye in Dover and saw ye leave heading north and west. He is still suspicious and is leadin' a group south, with Gaphard. They also saw ye alone. Where is Lady Victoria?"

Muttering a curse, he answered, "With Andrew. I knew when Phillip's ruffians saw me, they would give chase. I didn't want her in the midst of that."

"Why?" Her confused frown filled Dominic with a need to explain he couldn't quite understand himself. "They would not harm her. Dalmont would skewer any who tried."

"I cannot take that risk, not with her life," he rationalized. "After all, she is the most important element in my plan. I can have no revenge if she is dead."

Corinne nodded in concession. "Aye. Did her mum's death upset her?"

Dominic nodded, relieved their conversation was back on safe ground. "She was distraught, to say the least."

"Ye must understand that."

"Yes, but I hated to leave her grieving and alone."

She waved his concern away. "Andrew is with her. He will keep 'er safe and, more than like, amused."

Dominic paced the cobblestone in agitation, disliking the picture of Victoria amusing herself in Andrew's embrace that filtered across his mind. Feeling Corinne's gaze upon him, he stood still.

"Ye know he'll protect 'er, Nicky."

He paused. "He will keep her from harm."

"And 'e's got a rake's charm. She will likely enjoy herself."

Dominic's fists clenched at his sides at the thought. Corinne's gaze caught the gesture. Dread rose within him as she shot him a knowing stare.

"Ye fear he'll seduce 'er, don't ye?" she asked suddenly.

Startled to hear his fear spoken aloud, he let his gaze fly to her large liquid-brown eyes. He groped for an answer, one glib enough to turn the conversation elsewhere without suspicion. Nothing of the sort came to mind.

Finally, he whispered hoarsely, "He's been my friend, a man I've trusted with my life, since the night he smuggled me out of prison. But I do not trust him to leave Victoria untouched."

"Untouched? Nicky, ye make no sense. If ye've made 'er your mistress as planned, no doubt ye've bedded her a dozen times." She shrugged. "Allowin' Andrew to bed 'er might even be a better revenge, for it would eat at Dalmont's gut."

He rejected that notion instantly. "Perhaps, but such would be much too cruel to Victoria."

"What does it matter? She's simply a means to yer revenge."

"I cannot hurt her more than I have," he murmured.

"If Andrew seduces 'er gently, ye will have no more of her pain to worry about."

The thought, dear God, the vision, of *his* Victoria in Andrew's arms shafted Dominic with immediate pain—and the unsettling urge to throttle the man.

"Ye're frowning," Corinne said. "Fiercely, I might add. Would ye not allow Lady Victoria a lover?"

Dominic swallowed the truth. "Not until I release her. I don't need her romantic liaisons interfering with my plans."

During a long pause, Corinne studied his face. "No, there is more to yer fear, Nicky."

Christ, he thought, rubbing tired eyes. "My only fear is in failure to extract the best revenge possible."

Corinne pressed her lips to the underside of Dominic's chin. "If that's so and ye care nothing for 'er, then spend the night with me."

He shook his head, not even considering the notion. "I have no time for that."

Dominic stepped away, too afraid to examine the reason for his lie.

"Ye have ten minutes, surely. We could share our passions in the garden," she challenged. "We have before."

He stared into her familiar dark eyes, terrified to discover he could find none of the desire she usually ignited. "No."

"Why not? Because ye are thinking of Lady Victoria?"

Dominic turned his face from her, uncertain what to say when he could scarcely understand his feelings for Victoria himself.

"How often do ye make love to her?" Corinne asked.

Her tortured whisper twisted his insides. "Let's talk of something else. How is your sister?"

"How often, Nicky? Daily?" Her voice shook.

"Corinne, it's of no consequence." He stroked her shoulder in an attempt to soothe her.

She jerked from his touch. "It is! I've lost ye, I know. But why? Do ye bed her daily?"

Not certain what answer, if any, would mollify her, Dominic said nothing.

She gasped. "More than that?"

Prodded by the rising pain in her voice, Dominic grabbed Corinne's shoulders, willing her to listen and understand. "Be reasonable. You dislike the thought I've bedded Victoria and that I might find her desirable beyond my revenge. It gives me no comfort, either. But you and I have sought and shared only mutual pleasure. You never wanted me underfoot for long."

"But I 'ave always cared for ye," she argued. "I deserve the truth, Nicky. Do ye make love to 'er daily?"

"No." He closed his eyes against a rush of remembrances of soft skin, whispering sheets, urgent moans. He raked a trembling hand through his hair. "Damn it, we . . . It only happened once."

He opened his eyes and saw Corinne look away in anguish. "But ye desire only Lady Victoria now. Ain't that true?"

How could he answer? When he was with Victoria, he smelled her, tasted her skin, heard her laughter. When he was away from Victoria, her image swirled in his mind until he ached, body and soul.

"I can't help it." His words sounded raspy, even to his own ears. "She is not at all what I expected, what I was prepared for. She has me so confused . . ."

Corinne nodded tightly. "Do ye love her?"

Immediately, he opened his mouth to deny it, then paused. Did he? No answer echoed inside him. What did he know of love? Infatuation he understood, for Marcella had taught him that well enough. But what he felt for Victoria was different. It went deeper than that. Deeper than lust, certainly. Yet defining it seemed impossible. He admired the courage it must have taken her to threaten him, a towering stranger, with his own knife and to steal his keys. She was nothing like Marcella. She seemed more selfless, more genuine, as evidenced by her concern for her father during her own time of grief.

What *did* he feel for Victoria?

"Dominic? Do ye love 'er?" Corinne demanded.

Frustration and confusion racking him, he finally answered, "I don't know." Turning away, he cursed a short, brutal syllable. "I only know it scares the hell out of me."

Twelve

Victoria lifted her gaze from the canvas before her when she heard the sudden slam of the gate. She rose from her stool slowly, afraid to believe her ears. A fluttery feeling knotted in her stomach. Had Dominic finally returned?

She stepped to the canyon's entrance and found him standing there amidst the budding green-and-purple foliage, the setting sun casting his shadow over her. Without thought, she closed the distance between them, her heart racing like a horse at breakneck speed.

He looked like a bronzed god, tall and windblown. The gold in his eyes stood out like Spanish coins against his austere black shirt. The scents of damp earth, deep forest and all-male musk clung to him, reaching her on the humid air in an intoxicating drift. She ached to reach out, to welcome him back with a touch. Perdition, how she had missed him, even if it were foolish.

He returned her stare; his gaze flared hotter than a bonfire, engulfing her in their flames. Victoria recognized that look, the one that filled his eyes when they made love. Had he missed her, too?

"Dominic," she greeted him, her voice breathy.

"Victoria," he answered, his voice strangely husky.

She smiled, touching a hand to his shoulder. "Thank

goodness you're unharmed. I began to worry Dalmont had caught you."

He glanced at her hand on his arm, then at her face. At his sides, he formed fists. His jaw tightened; his eyes narrowed. The emotion in his hazel eyes vanished an instant later.

Leaning away from her touch, he intoned, "I am well, as you can see."

Confusion swirled through her at his sudden change. "Yes, you were gone longer than I expected. Where did you go?"

"I'm in one piece and unharmed. Beyond that, my travels are none of your concern. Do not play the nagging wife."

With that, he stepped around her and strode on. Pain seared within her, spreading, more intense than she'd known possible. No joy at their reunion; indeed, no emotion at all. He felt nothing for her—not contempt, not even pity.

Seconds later, she heard Andrew approach and greet Dominic. As she listened to Dominic's subdued reply, Victoria closed her eyes, feeling the impact of his deep-timbered voice within her. On long silent nights, she could almost hear the exquisite tenderness in his voice, his strong tones slurred with passion while he made love to her.

Her battered pride combating the urge to cry, she left the men, and Dominic's haunting voice, for the solitude of the pond. Somehow, she must hide her feelings. He could never know how deeply she cared for him, for Andrew had been right. Even if Dominic had any feeling for her at all, he would never show it.

And she was twice the fool for hoping otherwise.

* * *

"We must talk about Victoria," Andrew said once he and Dominic stood alone inside the cottage.

"Is she unwell?" Anxiety tightened a fist around Dominic's heart. He tried to disguise his reaction by turning away to set his saddlebags in the corner.

"She is perfectly well."

Then what did Andrew mean to say? Dominic couldn't stop his racing heart. Had Victoria succumbed to his friend's seduction? Had she enjoyed lying in the other man's arms?

Andrew continued, "I simply want you to be aware that, in your absence, Victoria acted differently than I expected."

"How so?" Tension tightened harder in his chest. He turned away to warm some coffee and indulge in a deep breath. Had Victoria's behavior been wanton? Or withdrawn?

"I thought she would be relieved you had gone, even if it were temporarily. She was quite the opposite, even expressing concern for your safety on more than one occasion."

She had truly worried about him. For some reason Dominic didn't want to examine too closely, that thought suffused warmth in the hollow where his heart had once lain. But tenderness and joy at their reunion were costly emotions to his restraint, ones he could ill-afford, particularly after the way Victoria had haunted his thoughts day and night these past four weeks. She was too close; his heart lay too exposed to resist the radiance of her warmth much longer. Pushing her away, evoking her hate—and locking away his own foolish, vulnerable wants—was his only chance for survival.

"What is your point?" Dominic demanded.

"Are you daft, man? She is in love with you."

Every nerve in his body froze. They were words he had considered—dreamed of—but hearing them aloud worked a terrifying effect all its own. Was it true? *Had* she found something beneath his rage to love? Despite himself, Dominic's heart thudded with hope, even as his mind damned the notion. She must not care for him; he must not allow her to tempt him from vengeance with the sunshine of her love.

"I cannot imagine why she has any feeling for you at all, since you've done little but manipulate her," Andrew added.

"Manipulate?" Dominic parried. "Not her heart. Not by design."

"Rubbish," Andrew growled. "You never do anything without a reason."

"Why would I seek Victoria's ardor? It bears no relevance to my plans and would only hurt her." Dominic gauged the skeptical expression crossing Andrew's rigid face. "I've indicated to her that any emotional attachment is unwise."

"To no avail. She loves you."

"That bothers you, I take it?"

"Of course," Andrew asserted. "You will never admit any such return of her sentiments, regardless of what may lie in your heart. Besides, this emotion is dangerous to your plan."

With a sigh, Dominic acknowledged Andrew's point. "In that, you are right."

"I do not like to see her hurt," Andrew added. "Dominic, she is . . . special to me."

Dominic's old jealousy flared to life with wild intensity. "Special?" He raised an accusing brow. "Is that how you refer to the women you try to conquer?"

"Dominic, listen to yourself. Your logic is lost in emotion as well. You have forgotten Victoria is your captive, not your woman. Not your wife."

Dominic clenched his jaw in silence, knowing unequivocally Andrew spoke true.

"What's this? Nary a word?" Andrew shot out.

"My sentiments are none of your concern. Nor are Victoria's. She is *my* captive, not your woman, either."

"Such hardly gives you free license to use her."

"But she will serve my purpose. And understand this now: If you've touched her, you never will again."

He'd voiced his worst fear; it was out in the open. Interminable heartbeats passed before Andrew responded, heartbeats that twisted his stomach in two.

"Bloody unbelievable! How can you accuse me of being too involved with Victoria when your jealousy is so strong, you can scarcely think of anything else?"

The accuracy of the statement only added fuel to Dominic's fury. "Did you touch her?"

He hesitated. "I will not answer that."

Dominic grabbed Andrew by the shirtfront, his lungs fighting for each breath, his chest constricting with unchecked rage. "Victoria is my concern, and I want an answer."

"She should be nothing to you but a means of revenge. Think, my friend, of your mission before it's too late."

Dominic released Andrew, who snapped his shirt back into place. "What do you care for my revenge? You never agreed with my methods."

"I agreed to help you. Think of what is most important—"

"Victoria is important, too, and I don't want you trifling with her."

"As if you haven't already?" Andrew snarled.

Dominic could scarce believe he was fighting with his only friend, that history seemed to be repeating itself. He felt powerless to stop their discord.

"You are free to leave anytime you wish"

Andrew squared his shoulders. "No, I gave my promise that I would help you. I always keep my word."

"If you truly want to help, then say no more about my connection with Victoria."

Andrew shook his head, his stare accusing. "If you're opposed to the truth, I shall say nothing more."

Dominic watched Andrew retreat, feeling their comfortable friendship shatter.

"Did the search parties spot you?" Andrew asked tightly across the table that evening.

Though Dominic had spread a sumptuous supper out before them, Victoria had hardly touched a bite. Instead, she stared at the fire snapping in the hearth, fearing that to look at Dominic would reveal the feeling in her heart to him.

"Yes," he answered slowly. "Three times."

"Did they give chase?"

"Naturally. They nearly caught me once." He shook his head. "If not for the dark, I would not have escaped."

Victoria's heart jumped in her throat. She told herself she shouldn't care if Dalmont's men recaptured Dominic, but that lump of fear stuck. She fought to set down her fork without a nervous, noticeable clang.

"Where are Dalmont's men now? Far away?" Victoria couldn't resist asking.

Dominic's suspicious gaze sliced to her. "Don't plan on seeing your betrothed soon. I will not give you or my revenge up that easily."

Andrew cleared his throat. "Dominic, you and I should alternate scouting the area, just to be certain we're safe. If you agree, I'll take the watch tonight so you can rest."

Dominic nodded. "Thank you."

Andrew waved his thanks away, then rose from the table. He took Victoria's hand in his and gave her knuckles a light brush with his lips. Then, to her utter shock, he smiled with mischief before turning her palm up and pressing his lips to the sensitive skin of her wrist.

"Until tomorrow, my lady."

After Andrew closed the door, a silence engulfed the one-room cabin until Dominic found it an unbearable abyss.

His gaze swerved to Victoria, watching as she bowed her head, ignoring him. The doubts he'd been trying to suppress rose to the surface to taunt him.

Had she, with hopes of escape, allowed Andrew to make love to her while he'd been away, running like the fox in a hunt? Was that how she had become "special" to his friend? He lifted her chin with tense fingers, raising her face to his, and stared into the fathomless blue depths of her eyes. He wondered if the longing he saw therein was for Andrew. Could her affections be as fickle and mercenary as Marcella's?

It doesn't matter, he told himself. She was nothing more than his captive—not his wife, nor even his mistress— and he wasn't concerned with her liaisons. *Liar.* The word echoed damningly through his soul.

He cursed. It *did* matter. She mattered. He wanted to brand her as his for all to see, for all time. The feeling seized his breath, shredded his guts, ate away at his heart. In his head, Corinne's memory asked him if he loved Victoria. Suddenly, he was afraid he knew the answer.

"What did you and Andrew do while I was gone?" He voiced the question casually, holding irrational accusations at bay.

She shrugged. "Nothing. I painted. He watched, and we talked."

"And what did you . . . talk about?"

She sliced her gaze to him. "Exactly what are you asking?"

"Well, you two seem to have grown close in my absence."

A frown pinched Victoria's red mouth. She looked so damned innocent, Dominic nearly swore. "You find that puzzling. I consider him a friend, much as he is to you."

"Friend?" Dominic parried. "Apparently more yours than mine, for he never kissed my wrist. But I can see why he might be partial to you."

"In what way?" Her voice rose in anger.

"Come now," he chided. "You're not obtuse."

Outrage flushed her delicate features as she gasped. "You may have the morals of a sewer dweller, but do not insinuate I'm your equal in that respect!"

A scowl thundered across Dominic's face. "It has little to do with morals and more to do with passion. I remember how easily and fully you succumb to it."

She shot him a frosty glare. "I hardly jumped into your bed the first moment I saw you. As I recall, I did very much to keep out of it."

He grasped her arm, acknowledging the gesture as a possessive one. "Even so, your reaction was complete."

Color climbed its way up her cheeks. "You will *never* see such a reaction from me again, I assure you."

"Don't be so sure."

Eyes flashing blue fire, she yanked her arm from his fingers. "That was not our bargain. You said once, one night in your bed. I fulfilled that obligation."

Victoria rose from the table and headed for the door—for Andrew, Dominic was sure. That possessive demon, now running hot and terrified, urged him to grab her wrist and pull her close.

"You're *mine*, Victoria."

She let loose a harsh laugh. "I mean no more to you than the dirt beneath your boots."

Dominic wanted to tell Victoria how wrong she was. He wanted to tell her he loved her as he cradled and comforted her in his arms—but he wasn't sure he could trust her with his heart. Such a confession was too dangerous, both to his mission and his soul. He would do well to remember that.

"Do you enjoy watching him use every ruse he knows to seduce you?" he demanded, knowing the knowledge might sear him.

"He would never do what you did," she insisted.

Dominic sucked in a hard breath. "Did he tell you he loves you? Were you naive enough to believe it?"

"You ordered me to stop playing the nagging shrew. Well, now you must heed your own advice and stop playing the jealous husband. You have no right to question what I do. Or with whom I do it."

"I'm making it my right."

His lips crashed down on hers. A flood of emotion burst past the remnants of its dam. Dominic held her tighter. His tongue invaded her mouth, yearning for her response.

She tore her lips away. "Stop it!'

"Stop what? Kissing you? Touching you?" he whispered. "Never."

He reached for her, then pulled her onto his lap so she straddled him. As the tip of his tongue touched her lower lip, he groaned at the sheer heaven of having her in his arms again.

Dominic teased her with biting kisses. "Did you know we could make love like this?"

She drew back from him, desire warring with anger and uncertainty on her sweet face. She tried to rise, but his hand at the swell of her bottom stayed her, fitting her against his aching arousal.

"Did you know that?" he repeated against her neck, his whisper intimate.

Her pulse began a nervous dance at the base of her throat, matching her shallow breaths. "Let me up."

"Aren't you curious?"

"No."

A cold rock of dread settled inside his chest as Dominic released her. "Because Andrew showed you?" The words were out before he could stop them.

"He did not touch me, nor did I invite him to." She sounded exasperated and angry. But that meant nothing. Marcella had continued to deny his suspicions until the day she'd left.

Dominic grabbed her arms. His brows vexed into a painful frown as he struggled to understand the emotions that drove him to this mad display of jealousy. He yearned to believe in her, to release the shackles of his distrust.

"Victoria, when I left three weeks ago, you were still shy in his presence. Now you allow him the familiarity of kissing your wrist. He gazes at you with pure lust. What conclusion should that lead me to?"

Her chin rose stubbornly. "That you are intent on making much out of nothing. We are friends, and he is concerned about me."

"If you believe that, you're a naive fool. With the slightest encouragement, he wouldn't hesitate to throw you on your back and mount you."

Outrage colored her voice and posture as she tore herself away from him. "He never touched me that way!"

Memories of Marcella's betrayal flashed in Dominic's mind. "I wish I could believe you."

Victoria awoke alone the following morning. Though she knew Dominic was taking his turn scouting the area for Dalmont's men, his absence seemed to represent his lack of trust—and it hurt. With a troubled mind, she rose and dressed.

When a knock sounded minutes later, she opened the cottage's door to Andrew, who immediately urged her outside into the morning sunshine. His anxious expression told her he was going to ask questions she had no wish to answer.

He placed his hands on her shoulders and ran them down her arms as if examining her. "I heard Dominic yell last night. Did he harm you?"

She sighed heavily. "Of course not."

"But he upset you again, didn't he? What did he say?"

She looked away, embarrassed. "I have little notion why, but he believes you and I are lovers."

Andrew nodded. "He'll believe it unless he has proof otherwise."

Her surprised gaze flew to him. "You knew that?"

When Andrew answered with a nod, she asked, "Why? I would love him if he would let me, but he keeps me outside his heart as though it were a fortress in need of protection."

"Don't expect differently. I fear he is not capable of love, my lady."

"Not capable?" Her voice reflected pain.

"Victoria, look at the man. He's too angry to give his love to anyone." He raised troubled eyes to her. "Is there any chance . . . of a child?"

She felt color rush to her cheeks. "No."

The tension left his bearded face. "Good. Perhaps if I ask Dominic to release you, he will."

"Release me?" She heard the shock in her voice and felt even greater shock when she wondered if she even wanted freedom anymore.

"Dominic might release you into my keeping."

Victoria could do nothing but blink at him for several weighted moments. To him? "He will never agree. Why would you ask such a thing?"

He stroked her cheek with his thumb, his blue-gray eyes locked with hers. "Dalmont is chasing Dominic hard and will catch him soon if he doesn't flee. You're not safe here, and the pace would be too taxing for you to go with him. Besides, Dalmont's men are dangerous. And with Dominic's irrational behavior, he is, too."

Victoria recognized Andrew's logic. But something inside her rebelled against that, resisted leaving Dominic.

"Oh, my lady." He lifted her hand and crushed it against his lips. "Can't you see I want to make you happy? That I love you no matter how I tried not to? I want your love in return."

Victoria stared at him in shock. "You love me?"

Andrew dropped to his knees. "With all my heart. From the moment I saw you." He grasped both her hands. "Oh, Victoria, let me show you the depth of my love."

She tried to withdraw her hands, but he held her tightly. "Show me?"

"Let me show you what it is like to be loved tenderly, not raped."

With a swallow of apprehension, she shook her head. "But—"

"Don't say no. Let me give you my love."

Victoria retreated a step. "Andrew, Dominic didn't rape me," she whispered. "I went very willingly."

"He threatened you with violence if you resisted."

Victoria shook her head. "No. I would have gone anyway, probably sooner if it hadn't been for his threats."

He rose and waved her words away. "That is in the past. Once you see how well I can love you—"

"No." She urged him to his feet, stopping his speech. "You deserve a woman whose heart belongs to you only. Right or wrong, mine belongs to Dominic."

"It won't forever," he insisted. "In time, you could feel more for me than you think you feel for him."

"Andrew, I—"

"Let me show you. Please." His cajoling eyes matched his tone.

Was Andrew right? Could she ever love him? Did he love her in a way Dominic was not capable of?

Andrew leaned toward her. She knew his intent, and allowed his warm lips to move over hers. He kissed her softly at first, without demand. His lips brushed over hers, evoking nothing except guilt and the uncomfortable urge to push him away.

"You aren't like other women," he whispered against her mouth. "You are sweet and trusting, and you fill me with such desire . . ."

His mouth descended on hers again. This time, his tongue lunged between her lips, thrusting into her mouth. Alarmed by his sudden force, her hands flew to his shoulders and she tried to push him away.

"I need you, my lady," he whispered, wedging himself closer to her. "Let me show you."

He lifted her against his chest, crushing her frantic hands between them, then settled her on the ground, his big body smothering her. As she writhed for freedom, dew from the grass seeped a cold wetness into her clothing, chilling her skin. Cool air hit her thighs as he lifted her skirt. His callused palm covered her tender flesh a moment later.

"Andrew, I beg you—"

"I know, love," he crooned, subduing her struggles with a strong embrace. "I am impatient, too."

Panic set in as Victoria realized Andrew actually thought her willing. She squirmed beneath him more, desperately seeking escape, but his determination held her.

He ripped away the first three buttons of her dress. "Andrew, please! I'm—"

"Hush, my lady. You will enjoy it." His teeth grazed her neck. Victoria felt each touch like a razor. "I promise."

"No, she won't!" Dominic suddenly snarled.

Then he charged toward Andrew.

Thirteen

Andrew rolled away and jumped up like a startled cat. With a cry of relief, Victoria sprang to her feet and swung her gaze to Dominic. She wanted to cry out, to thank God for sending him to save her.

His savage expression froze the words in her throat.

Frightening rage tightened every contour of his face, emphasizing his rigid jaw and the fury blazing in his gold-green eyes. His arms trembled as his fists clenched in silent testimony to his anger. A wide-legged stance conveyed quiet menace and an urge to fight.

"Swine!" Dominic's growl rent the powerful hush.

Andrew held up his hands in placation. "Before you lose your temper, think of Victoria, of what she needs. You can't give her the attention she deserves."

"That is between Victoria and me!"

Charging at Dominic, Andrew snarled, "Damn it! You cannot make her happy."

Dominic's eyes narrowed as Andrew stopped before him. "Oh, and you can? Bloody hell, what do you have to offer her?"

"I am not too cowardly to tell her I love her."

Dominic curled his fists at his sides. "Love is something you conveniently confuse with lust when a fair lady listens. At least I never led her to believe I would show her everlasting devotion."

"No, you simply used her like a common whore," Andrew countered. "Only you paid her in cruelty, not coins."

Dominic reached out and grabbed Andrew by the throat. "Get out."

His voice resonated with a rage that made Victoria shiver. The men faced each other. Anger and animosity thrummed between them, producing a thick mixture of volatility. Victoria saw Dominic's fury heightening in every inch of his taut stance.

While he and Andrew exchanged glances promising pain and retribution, terror surged within her. Victoria feared that, in this rage, either man could be capable of any kind of violence.

She tried to catch the gazes of both men with her pleading eyes. Neither returned her stare. Dominic's frigid scowl, black brows slashing in harsh fury, dashed her hopes for peace.

Suddenly, she heard a primal scream shatter the silence as Dominic charged. Andrew answered with a curse, fists raised. The sickening sound of fists connecting with flesh made her stomach turn as Andrew's head snapped back. A rush of guilt, followed closely by anger, rushed through her. The metallic tinge of blood scented the air. Her stomach pitched in protest.

Andrew's jab, aimed at Dominic's jaw, found his shoulder instead. Dominic shrugged the blow away, then slammed a punishing fist into Andrew's stomach. He fell to his knees.

"Stop it! Both of you!" Victoria screamed.

They cast their startled gazes in Victoria's direction.

Their faces were red and swollen. A trickle of blood trailed from the corner of Andrew's mouth.

"See what you've done to each other!" She turned upheld hands and desperate eyes to Dominic. "Though I did not want Andrew, he did not hurt me. Is that what you want to hear?"

Eyes narrowed upon her, Dominic released the other man. Andrew stood slowly, holding his head in his hands. Victoria watched him rise unsteadily.

"Dominic is right. You should go." Her voice shook as she spoke to the man she had once thought her friend. Relief and fury pumped through her body, making her legs tremble as well.

"And what of you?" Andrew asked.

"I shall stay."

He paused, looking from her to Dominic, who had moved to stand just inches behind her in a possessive gesture. "If that is your wish."

She glanced over her shoulder, drinking in the safety of Dominic's silent, stoic presence. "Indeed, it is. Good-bye."

Within minutes, the gate's slam reverberated through the ravine with a *clank* Victoria felt all the way to her heart. After an agonizing moment, the crunch of Dominic's returning footsteps reached her ears, sounding like a death march. As Dominic burst through the wild thyme and birch trees, he seemed to seethe. He passed her in silence, making his way to the cottage.

His icy rage sent chills through her. She followed him, not knowing what to say or do.

He speared her with a furied glance as she entered the little domain. Wisely, Victoria held her tongue and turned to the hearth. Dominic slammed the cottage door so violently the walls shook. The sound echoed in her ears. Her entire being leapt with trepidation and fury.

When she turned to face him, Victoria saw the white-hot anger branding his face, mixed with a fear she didn't understand. His knuckles, still clenched at his sides, were dotted with drying blood. Andrew's blood. Blood he had lost because of her.

Victoria resisted the nausea bobbing in her stomach and faced Dominic with bravado. "Dominic, I—"

"Not now."

He turned his back to her and sloshed brandy into a tin cup. Raising the mug to his mouth, he downed the contents in one quick swallow.

Victoria watched, torn between concern and fright. Clearly, he thought her a willing partner to Andrew. Yet how could he after the special night she had spent wrapped in his embrace?

"Yes, now," she demanded. "Right this instant, you lout!"

Dominic whipped his gaze to her. His eyes glittered dangerously, cheekbones slashing on either side of his face like angry blades.

"Lout? At least I didn't find myself beneath a complete cad with my skirts rucked up about my knees."

She shot him a narrow-eyed glare. "Yes, I'm certain it is my fault for not possessing the strength to ward off someone twice my size."

"It works better if you at least try," he said, his glare wry.

Victoria threw her hands up in exasperation. "I refuse to talk to you when you cannot see sense."

"Does the truth hurt too much?" He grabbed her arm.

She jerked away from his grip. "No, only the fact you seem determined to cast me in Marcella's mold. How can you believe that of me?"

He turned away. Silence ensued. Victoria stared at the breadth of Dominic's tense shoulders, watched his long-legged pacing with a shiver.

Finally, he turned, his stare piercing her with anger, fear, and lust at once. "I cannot believe I let this happen again, your little *amor*. After all that planning . . ." His laugh sounded self-deprecating as he faced her again. "And with my only friend. I do seem to have a knack for losing women to those I trust."

"Lose me? As if you ever wanted me for anything other than revenge? As if you ever bloody cared about me?" Her voice rose with each word.

He snaked a hand about her nape, pulling her face inches beneath his. "Oh, I care," he whispered against her mouth. "To the point of folly."

Victoria's heart stopped for an instant before she realized that to believe him would be the greatest folly ever.

"That is a lie," she accused. "I yielded my body to you out of genuine desire. You came to me with only revenge in your heart."

"I should have." His voice grew raspy as he shook his head. "But the night we spent together . . . God help me, how I wanted you."

"You treated me so cruelly afterward as a means of desiring me further?" Sarcasm dripped from each word. She refused to believe him, no matter how much she yearned to.

A possessive fire illuminated Dominic's green-gold eyes. "How else was I to keep my word to bed you just once? My only hope was to make you despise me."

She scowled. "That is completely illogical."

His gaze invaded her soul. "Is it? No matter how much I've rationalized, denied, or lied, the truth is I want you. I wanted you again ten minutes after we made love." His voice dropped another octave. "I want you now."

His mouth covered hers, not with the fierce taking she expected. Instead, she encountered a pleading, a coaxing—a surprisingly vulnerable quality that nearly made her heart stop.

He held her urgently, as if afraid to let go. His mouth stroked hers almost reverently, his taste of coffee and despair. An answering surge of desire moved through her. She reached for him as he nibbled her lips, held her close, whispered her name.

Finally, he rested his forehead against hers. "I will not share you."

"Dominic, I did not *seek* Andrew's passion," Victoria whispered. "I am not Marcella."

"No," he said huskily. "You confuse me, make me want you and hate you all in the same breath."

He claimed her mouth again, urging her lips apart with a provocative persuasion that made her head spin and reality recede. Clinging to his shoulders, her anchor in the spinning world of desire, she moaned as his tongue swirled with her in a soft seduction she could barely find the strength to fight.

With the last vestige of her resistance, she broke off their kiss with a turn of her head. She pushed against his chest, desperately needing space between them, for she knew that his kiss, coupled with his earthy musk, could swamp her senses into submission.

"Victoria," he protested, voice raspy with passion. "I won't hurt you."

Despite his solemnity, she shook her head. "You will. You always do. You think of nothing but hate and revenge."

"Right now, I can think of nothing but you."

His words were so tempting, but most likely untrue. "Of satisfying your base needs with my convenient body?"

"I had a convenient opportunity for release while I was away." He sidled closer, dangerously close now. "I refused her. I want *you.*"

Surprise flickered through Victoria, even as hope eked its way through her heart. As he stood a bare inch from her, his scent awashed her senses again, a heady mix of earth and man—and arousal. Desire curled insidiously in her belly. She had no notion where she would find the strength to resist him.

"You and I, we want each other," he asserted softly.

Victoria tried to shake her head in denial. Dominic caught her cheek with his palm. His skin was a warm comfort on her clammy, flushed face.

"I won't lie to myself anymore," he said. "Rational or not, I want you. Look inside yourself. Your eyes tell me you feel the same desire."

He was right, she thought. Dear God, he was right. Victoria closed her eyes, torn between the warnings in her head and the urgings of her heart.

Suddenly, she felt his fingers, feather light, trail down her sensitive inner arm. He took her hand in his a moment later, and Victoria opened her eyes just in time to watch him take her mouth in another kiss that made her soul his gentle prisoner.

Sweet Mary, she ached. Wanted him beyond reason as she returned the kiss with all her pent-up desire. He responded with a moan as his lips blazed a trail down her cheek to her neck. There, his mouth made a welcome invasion of her responsive flesh.

Tangling her hands in his dark hair, she urged him closer, rolling her head aside to allow his lips room to roam. And roam they did, all the way to the upper swells of her breasts. His breath hot against her skin, he laved her with kisses, his hands urging her breasts upward toward his waiting mouth.

She loved the way he wanted her. She loved the way he made her feel beautiful and wanton.

She loved him.

Unable to hold herself back, she covered his neck with kisses of her own. At her sensual assault, he hissed in a sharp breath.

"Yes," he encouraged. "Yes."

Their mouths met again for a fierce mating, this one demanding the full measure of her passion. Victoria answered, meeting the unabashed thrust of his tongue, even as she drowned in a heavy sea of desire.

Dominic yanked the tails of his shirt free from his breeches. The minute he bared his skin, she touched her lips to his chest, wanting to lay claim to him, to his heart. Tracing his shoulder with her tongue, she caressed the expanse of his back with her hands.

His touch was a hot delight Victoria knew would lead her to heaven. With a gentle tug, Victoria pulled his shirt over his head and tossed it to the ground.

As he murmured his appreciation in an unintelligible syllable and caressed her in return, her breathing grew labored. She was long past the point of mere arousal. Every whisper-light touch of his fingers across her skin seemed its own exquisite torture.

"This is madness." Her voice carried breathy need.

Dominic grazed her tender neck with his lips. "This is wonderful."

Victoria attempted to murmur a response—only to find her words trapped in her throat by his fingers skimming the sensitive surface of her nipples with his thumbs.

From there, his hands glided over her buttocks and the sides of her thighs. Closer, closer . . . his body pressed hotter, harder, against hers until she trembled beneath his touch.

"Why can't I stay away from you?" she asked, voice choked.

"Or I from you?" he returned in soft rhetoric.

Their gazes clashed, and Victoria realized the futility of fighting a yearning that had grown bigger than both of them.

He demolished the row of buttons down the back of her dress and lifted it from her, never once looking away. With a flick of his wrist, it joined his shirt on the floor, utterly forgotten. As she hoped, Dominic began raising her chemise. He stopped just below her breasts.

His thumbs brushed over the linen-covered velvet nubs of her nipples. Arching into him, she clutched his wrists as he urged the chemise higher yet.

"Please . . ."

"Please make love to you?" he murmured against her neck. "Give you pleasure?" His gaze captured hers. "Touch you until you can scarcely breathe?"

Her breath caught on a gasp as she tried to speak. "Yes."

He waited no further. The cadence of his harsh breathing echoed in her ears, just like the pounding of her heart. The insistent smell of arousal blanketed them. The sight of him, half-naked and wanting, made her insides beat with wild desire.

"Last time, I held back for fear of hurting you. This time, I'll hold nothing back."

Dominic's mouth descended and found hers as he raised the chemise over her head. Hungry, insistent, he devoured the sweetness of her mouth, coaxing, giving. Victoria answered uninhibitedly.

His hands roamed down her back, across her buttocks. His tense fingers clenched her hips, fitting her against him intimately. Warmth and tingles besieged her. She responded with a cry.

His hands were greedy as they worked their way up her back, around her shoulders, and finally to her breasts. He skimmed his thumbs across her taut nipples again. She melted against him as he backed her against the nearest wall. Dropping to his knees before her, he glanced up into her passion-flushed face, then lowered his gaze again to regard what was directly before him: the joining of her thighs.

She understood his intent and tried to step away. His hands clutched her hips, impeding her retreat.

"Dominic, I—"

"I told you I would hold nothing back," he interrupted. "For three hellish weeks I've abstained from touching you. Each day I did, I had more time to fantasize just how I would make love to you."

With that, he lifted her thigh to his mouth and kissed it, his lips moving outside, along her hip. Then he forged a new path; his lips, teeth, and tongue worked together, moving upward and inward.

Suddenly his mouth was but a breath away from her moist secrets. Her legs were weak; her hands trembled.

Her fast, shallow breaths did nothing to cure the mists of desire ruling her head.

Both triumph and tenderness infused his expression as he placed her leg over his shoulder, her calf dangling down his back.

Victoria swallowed hard as he placed the softest kiss against her abdomen. Her stomach quivered beneath his lips, and pulsed again when he gathered her buttocks in his palms and tilted her hips toward his mouth.

At the first touch of his lips against the bud of her desire, she cried out, hands grasping his shoulders for support. Again, his mouth closed around the sensitive nub, sending a second wave of reaction ricocheting through her.

His kisses grew stronger, his tongue and teeth bolder as he laved and suckled her without haste. Victoria felt herself dissolving under his touch, felt the real world dwindling away.

Sparks and stars danced in her vision, swirling in her head like the brightest fireworks. Need churned in her belly, completely lacking mercy.

Suddenly, the desire within her expanded, then exploded. With the sound of her own pleasure in her ears and the feel of his flesh beneath her nails, she let endless ripples of pleasure wash through her, one after the other.

As the tumult subsided, he eased her into his arms and carried her to the bed with the care a mother would show her newborn babe. As he set her down, trailing kisses up her body, his hand skimmed her abdomen before rising to circle her nipple to a hard, aching point.

Victoria lay before him, spent yet aroused, as the

golden dusk beamed inside. She met his gaze. His expression screamed of unsatisfied desire.

Fingers tangling in the hair at his nape, she lifted herself into his kiss. Her tongue touched his with a fervency that seemed to send his passions into a tempest.

His frenzied fingers dropped to the buttons of his breeches and worked at them impatiently. Her hands joined his and succeeded where his trembling fingers failed. Together, they pushed and tugged until his breeches lay on the floor in a discarded heap.

Clamoring need was etched across his face as he lowered his head to nibble her bottom lip, evoking her passion.

When he moved to cover her body with his, she thrust her hands up to his chest, preventing it. With a gentle push, she urged him onto his back and rose above him with a provocative smile.

"Remember when you said we could make love like this?" she whispered.

The flame in his eyes flared to new heights, thrilling Victoria further. "With you atop? Oh, yes."

"Show me."

She leaned down to capture his mouth, and he reached for her like a starving man. With the feel of their mouths mating, he guided himself to her, placed his hands on her hips, and drew her down. A bevy of tingles leapt to life where they joined.

Steely and strong, he filled her in an exquisite union that was both heaven and hell, a bittersweet homecoming. She gasped, then arched, infused with pleasure, with need.

Beneath her, Dominic used his hands at her hips as a silent teacher. Fingernails biting into his skin, she clutched his wrists and took over, setting a slow, erotic pace. She rose, nearly allowing him to withdraw, then closed around him with a lack of haste that drove them both mad with need.

Soon her rhythm quickened, and with it, her breathing. In the dying sunlight, she watched the expressions of pleasure-pain cross his unforgettable face.

Faster and higher, her movements drove them toward heaven. She felt the crescendo within her building, escalating to exhilarating heights.

Dominic suddenly rolled her to her back and allowed her no time to question why before he drove deep inside her. Fitting his hands beneath her hips, he established his own rhythm, hard and insistent.

As she lifted herself to him, her breathing quickened into shallow gasps. With frenzied movements, she met his every thrust until she quivered and tightened around him in an explosion that surpassed the first.

His gaze captured hers as her body yielded to pleasure. With her cry on the air between them, he surrendered his control, his moan of release echoing in the warm cottage air.

Long moments later, he rolled to his side and cuddled her against his damp chest. The sheets rustled, soft as a lover's whisper. The following silence seemed to say what no words could, permeating her with a blinding bolt of love. She placed tiny, weary kisses across his chest. Absently, he stroked her hair.

Her gaze locked with his, taking in his sated face and damp brow. She yearned to tell him she had felt their souls merge and found the experience more beautiful than any other. Yet she felt more . . . more that boiled down to three simple words she could not hold back.

"I love you."

* * *

Dominic stared at Victoria, his heart somewhere near his throat. Of its own volition, his arm tightened about her waist. Sweet Jesus, how he yearned to believe she returned his feelings, even for a moment. But in his world, earl's daughters didn't pledge their hearts to wanted criminals. Men of honor, especially men with nothing to offer, did not trespass on a woman's heart, even if her vow amounted to nothing more than momentary fancy. And men seeking revenge resisted any such deviation from purpose.

Good arguments, all. So why did he want to tell her that he loved her, too? Impossible. What if she sought marriage? Given how much it had hurt to see her in Andrew's arms, and hurt in a way that Marcella's perfidy never had, Dominic feared the end of her feeling for him would be too much to bear. He refused to take that risk.

The sun sank below the horizon, leaving behind a fiery beam of brilliant orange-pink streaming into the cottage. He sighed heavily.

"You mistake the truth of it." He eased away from her to don his breeches.

Victoria sat up and drew her legs up to her bare chest, protecting her breasts from his gaze. "In what way?"

"Lust can be powerful, indeed, but it is still merely lust."

"Merely lust?" she shouted, leaving the bed to snatch her dress from the wooden floor. She swore when a sliver buried itself beneath her finger. Clutching the dress against her nakedness, she sucked her injured finger. "Lust cannot make my heart ache."

He shrugged in feigned indifference. "It might."

"Lust cannot make me trust you with my very life."

Uncertain if she truly meant that, Dominic stared.

Her expression showed no deceit, no uncertainty. He shook his head to clear it of such fanciful wishing.

"Lust would induce you to trust me, temporarily at least."

"That may be so, you foolish, stubborn man! But lust cannot make me yearn to bear your children and grow old with you."

No, it could not, he conceded. Infatuation could make one have those delusions for a time, however. But what if her love were genuine?

"Why do you refuse to believe me?" she asked.

There were so many reasons, he could hardly name one. Still, he chose the one that would drive him from her heart the fastest.

"Because I have no need for such love ever again, given the fact it bloody nearly killed me the first time."

The sound of Victoria's gasp was smothered by a loud bang above the canyon.

Musket fire, Dominic guessed from the ricochet. Damn! The retort echoed again, loud and booming. For a terrifying moment, he froze. *Please God, let it be hunters.* But the sinking stone of dread within his belly told him otherwise.

Icy with panic, Dominic rushed out of the cottage to the stable and grabbed his rifle. When he returned to Victoria's side, weapon in hand, he ordered, "Follow me—quietly."

Together, they crept outside, to the gate. A sweat broke out across his skin. Victoria followed, thankfully silent.

They paused at the gate. From behind the camou-flage of wild brambles, they stared out at the ground above them, Dominic trying to determine the source of the gun blast.

Within moments, a lone man on a horse came trotting by, holding a dead rabbit by its ears.

Dominic's arm tightened around Victoria's waist in an unconscious gesture of possession when he saw the rider's face: Lord Gaphard.

He resisted the urge to swear. There was no use denying further that his ploy in Dover had been an unmitigated failure.

Biting his lip, Dominic glanced at Victoria in trepidation. He should send her back to the cottage. Here, fifty feet separated her from freedom. With one cry, she could return to her privileged, titled world and have her own revenge against his callous treatment of her by ensuring his death.

Could he trust her? Of course she'd professed her love and trust of him. He feared, however, her sentiment was nothing more than passing sentiment, as Marcella's had been. Given a choice, would she choose to remain with him or return to respectability and become a true duchess, as Marcella had craved to be?

"Is it one of the search parties?" she whispered.

The muscle in his jaw worked. Bracing himself for any of her responses, he gave her a silent nod.

She looked up into his face with pleading eyes, squeezing his hand between hers. "Do not let them find me. Please! I can no longer marry Dalmont."

For a long moment, he didn't move as relief and another warmer, more dangerous emotion flooded every corner of his body. At her waist, his hand tightened, bringing her closer to him, if only for a moment. "Do not worry, my lady. I won't."

Dominic's gaze returned to the spot where Gaphard had been. Moments later, to his horror, Phillip Dowling, the duke of Dalmont himself, trailed behind Lord Gaphard. Beside him, Victoria smothered a gasp with her hand.

He looked the same as always: arrogant and cruel. The false halo of blond curls, the straight carriage, the thin mustache, the fashionable French coat belling out from waist to knee; none of it had changed. The mere sight of him made Dominic tremble with violence. Somehow, he maintained restraint.

They crouched that way for what seemed hours. When the party had ridden out of sight and the air around them lay quiet, Dominic rose and bid Victoria to do the same. Together they walked to the cottage, enveloped in silence.

At the threshold, Victoria paused. She reached for Dominic, but he stepped away, knowing all he'd planned for—all he wanted—would never be his. All he could do now was ensure the preservation of her life . . . and his own heart.

He turned to her, his expression carefully blank. "Pack your things, Victoria. We leave in one hour."

Fourteen

December, 1751
six months later

Perched upon a bench in the courtyard of the Pembridge School for Orphans, Victoria eyed the bare trees, stripped of their leaves by an earlier frost. She shifted little Callie on her lap and moved a stray lock of blond hair from the girl's eyes, then returned her attention to the gathering of wide-eyed children before her.

"Read it again, Ben," she instructed. "This time, think carefully about how you accent your words. French is pronounced differently than English."

The young boy read the line slowly and clearly, if not perfectly. Victoria congratulated him on his improvement.

At that moment, Callie squirmed impatiently, reminding Victoria that the hour designated for the French lesson was over. She closed the book and set it on the cobblestone by her feet.

"That is enough for today. By tomorrow, think of an entire sentence in French that describes your surroundings. Now, run to lunch."

With pride, she watched the twelve children of various ages scramble away across the stone floor, illuminated by the watery English sunshine. She marveled that they shared a common enthusiasm for learning, despite their differences.

"I'm hungry," Callie cried, interrupting her thoughts.

"And so we shall eat," Victoria promised, anchoring the youngest orphan, who was not yet three, on her hip, and headed for the kitchen.

To her left, the headmistress, Mrs. Youngston, opened her door and stepped into the courtyard in a swish of blue skirts. "Victoria, come quickly. I must speak with you."

Concern showed in the tense lines around the older woman's mouth, alerting Victoria that something was, indeed, amiss. "Of course. As soon as I feed Callie, I shall return at once."

Mrs. Youngston shook her graying head. "Let Mary feed her. What I must say is most important."

Dread winding through her veins, a terrible possibility occurred to Victoria. "Have I been found?"

The headmistress paused. "Just give Callie to Mary and come to my rooms."

Victoria frowned at the evasion in her employer's gaze. What if the odious Dalmont had found her? She had no wish to see the man, much less wed him.

Concern permeated her every nerve as she dashed away. Rushing through the familiar, narrow halls to the kitchen, Victoria found Mary within. After handing the child to the other teacher, she retraced her path across the courtyard, then dashed up the sun-washed stone steps to Mrs. Youngston's door.

Victoria entered breathlessly, without knocking. Distress whipped inside her. "Tell me. What's amiss?"

Mrs. Youngston gestured to a dark, spindle-backed chair before the desk. Quickly, Victoria took it.

The older woman bowed her head for a moment, steepling her slender fingers in thought. Finally, she regarded Victoria with a stoic stare. That solemn expression churned Victoria's stomach with a sudden, sick dread.

"I received a letter today." Mrs. Youngston paused, as if weighing her next words. "From Dominic Grayson."

Victoria felt the blood drain from her face. *Dear God. Yes!* her heart shouted. *No!* logic responded with equal ferocity.

She'd had absolutely no contact with him for the past six months—not since the morning he'd deserted her like some five-pence whore. Why had he written now?

Victoria didn't intend to subject herself to him and his deceit again simply to find out. She had made a fool of herself by telling Dominic she loved him. He had shunned her feelings with laughable ease, leaving her certain he cared enough to be possessive, as one would of property, but no more.

Victoria leapt from her seat. Mrs. Youngston's voice stayed her. "Please, sit. Hear what I have to say."

She felt the strength and confidence she'd spent the last six months assembling fray at the edges. She had taught twelve children the fundamentals of reading, art, French, and mathematics since coming here and was proud of her accomplishments. But this was the weak spot in her newfound armor; *he* was her vulnerability.

"I've no wish to talk about that man," she said stiffly.

"If I did not feel it was important, I would not ask you to listen." Mrs. Youngston paused. "For me, please."

Reluctantly, Victoria perched on the edge of her chair.

The woman began, "In this letter, Dominic says he is coming here—within the week."

Convulsively, Victoria shook her head, wishing she could deny the older woman's words. *Here? Within the week?* The thought filled her with both anticipation and panic. "Why?"

"He did not say."

With a deep breath, Victoria gathered her bravado. "I won't see him. I have no need to." *To subject myself to his mesmerizing charm, to open myself up to hurt once again.*

"Victoria, he would not return here unless his purpose was important."

"Why should I care for his purpose? He is not my husband or guardian, so he cannot force his presence on me. Tell him I simply refuse to see him."

"I won't do that." Mrs. Youngston's pause hung between them, heavy and tense, arousing Victoria's unease. "Dominic is like my own son. I very nearly raised him."

Victoria flew from her chair, anger and disbelief mingling within into a volatile mix. "So you've told me. But I believed you to be *my* friend as well. Clearly, I was mistaken."

Mrs. Youngston lifted her hands in a gesture of supplication. "Please, child. I truly care for you. But Dominic says it is imperative you see him."

Her words sent Victoria's temper reeling higher and faster. "Imperative to his plans, perhaps, but not mine!"

"I know he did not handle your earlier acquaintance in the best way possible," Mrs. Youngston cajoled, "but—"

"He abducted me," Victoria corrected. "From my

bed, in the middle of the night, and threatened to rape me."

The older woman cleared her throat in obvious discomfort. "Well, I know he had compelling reasons for such behavior."

"None of which make his actions acceptable." Putting a rein on her temper, Victoria shook her head. "I realize you care for him. But the way he treated me . . . I could tell you the cruel things he did to me, but I fear you'd never believe it."

"He admitted to abducting you," the older woman offered.

Victoria frowned in contempt. "That was the pleasant part."

Lips pursed, she murmured, "He did confess to seducing you."

The blood left Victoria's face in a cold ebb, then rushed back in rage and mortification. Whom else had he told of their intimacies? That he'd shared the truth with anyone told her he thought of her as little more than a doxy.

"That swine!"

"He very much needed the confession." Mrs. Youngston placed a bony hand on Victoria's shoulder. "It weighed upon his mind."

"He should have visited his parson instead," she said through gritted teeth.

"Dominic told me he regretted treating you as he did."

"Forgive me if I cannot believe such rubbish," she shot back.

"You should believe it," Mrs. Youngston whispered. "I think he loves you."

Victoria backed away from the woman with the spring

of a cornered feline. "Dominic seduced then discarded me. He left me here with strangers in the middle of the night without so much as a by-your-leave. Such displays of affection are near smothering, wouldn't you agree?"

The older woman's sigh held resignation. "Please understand that his experience with women has not been entirely favorable."

"I know about Marcella, and while I think her behavior was deplorable, that does not justify what he did to me."

"Of course not," Mrs. Youngston soothed. "But Lady Marcella shattered his trust, and he's allowed no one close enough to help him rebuild it."

"So, I am to acquiesce to the wishes of a single letter, not even addressed to me, and allow him to disrupt the peace I have found these last six months?"

Mrs. Youngston shook her head. "If Dominic wishes to see you, I cannot deny him. What you tell him is your own choice."

"Splendid. I shall refuse him myself."

"Why?" The question was a preamble to a soft, knowing silence. "I think you love him, too."

Victoria's blue eyes met the woman's dark ones. "I do *not* love him. Not anymore."

Mrs. Youngston closed the space between them in two steps. She placed motherly hands on Victoria's shoulders. "Look deep inside, beyond the hurt, behind the wall you've built around your heart. You'll find your love beating strongly. I see it in your face when you think no one is looking. I've seen the drawings of him you keep in your room."

Victoria's guilty gaze skittered away. Heat crept up her cheeks. She'd drawn Dominic in moments of passion, of anger and contentment. Yet she had not been able to purge him from her mind. There, he lurked each day during church, each night in her solitary bed as she ached for his touch. None of that, however, was love.

Was it?

Too afraid to answer her own question, Victoria looked pleadingly at Mrs. Youngston. "I—I can't see him."

"You must. I'm certain only you can persuade him to give up this foolish revenge."

With disbelieving eyes, Victoria stared back at Mrs. Youngston. "No one can persuade him to do that, least of all me. Please do not make me see the man I've spent six months learning to forget."

"You wasted time on hate instead of searching your heart for forgiveness and love."

Victoria shook her head. "He has none of those to give." Her voice shook as tears moistened her eyes. "Neither do I."

With that, Victoria whirled about, leaving Mrs. Youngston's office for the solace of her room.

Ignoring the cold stone bench beneath her, Victoria could only feel dread at the thought of confronting Dominic. She could scarcely sleep or eat. Concentration seemed beyond her, and she resented that fact. Where was all the indifference she had worked so hard to achieve?

Dear God, what would Dominic himself do to her emotions? Taking in the scent of dew-damp grass with her deep inhalation, Victoria tried to calm her wild thoughts.

Yesterday, Mary had suggested she was irritable. Mrs. Youngston had been more diplomatic and termed her behavior as preoccupied. Perdition, both of them were right. No matter how hard she tried to master her emotions, the tumult had invaded her like an incurable disease.

In the four days since Mrs. Youngston had told her of the letter, Victoria had tried to anticipate how she would react when Dominic arrived. Certainly not with joy. But if he whispered to her and held her in his arms? She would resist. His pretty words were lies; his every kiss was poison designed to sap her logic. She knew that now.

Six months ago, she had been gullible, much too innocent. Dominic had cured her of such vulnerabilities. Time and distance had given her the opportunity to see how easily he had lured her into his web of charm and deception. When he had abandoned her to the strangers at the orphanage, her pride had finally refused to allow her to care for him anymore. In no other way could he have told her so completely that he felt nothing for her. And so she felt nothing for him.

But some nights, like the last one, seemed too long for her betraying body. She'd lain awake, craving his nearness. She felt certain her reaction stemmed from an absence of physical contact any man could have assuaged. Still, the longings cast her into an abyss of despair, because she always dreamed of Dominic.

Rising, she began to pace the courtyard, hardly aware of the winter air swirling around her, lifting tree branches stripped of their leaves. Sweet mercy, *why* was he returning? Certainly not to extract further revenge upon Phillip by luring her to his bed again.

That possibility sent her into fury. *She* would decide the course of her life from now on, not Dominic. And neither he nor Dalmont were part of her plan.

"You seem unsettled," Mrs. Youngston commented, entering the barren courtyard. "Because of Dominic's arrival?"

"Why would you think that?" Victoria asked, turning her guilty gaze to the winter-frozen garden.

Mrs. Youngston shrugged. "It would be natural."

The older woman sat on the stone bench and gestured Victoria to do the same. Reluctantly, she did as the headmistress bid.

"Once, I loved a man," began Mrs. Youngston, her expression surprisingly wistful. "But he favored my sister, who was by far the prettier."

"Then he was a fool to look past all your qualities."

With a rueful smile, the woman went on. "While they courted, he never knew how I felt. I was too cowardly to tell him." The headmistress wrapped her arms about herself. "He often spoke to me, even danced with me once or twice. Every time I saw him, my stomach churned and my pulse raced. I could scarcely speak. So you see, I remember what it was like to be near the man I loved."

"I do not love Dominic."

Mrs. Youngston's glance was full of reproach. "So stubborn. If you do not tell him of your feelings, you will lose him. I never told my beloved, so he married my sister. Only upon his deathbed did he confess that he had loved me all along. If I had only told him what was in my heart, he would have wed me."

Victoria set her jaw in anger. "Well, I told Dominic I loved him once, to which he replied I could not discern the difference between lust and love. Then he left me. Now may we change the subject?"

Mrs. Youngston grimaced. "Mary said you've been short-tempered of late."

"I am simply tired."

Mrs. Youngston smiled slyly. "What bothers you more: the thought of seeing him or not knowing his intent?"

"I care nothing for the man or his plans."

The older woman went on as if Victoria hadn't spoken. "Dominic's letter was urgent, but somewhat vague, so I know nothing of his purpose." She shrugged. "I suppose you shall have to let him explain."

Victoria set her lips in a belligerent line. "I prefer not to listen to anything he has to say."

Mrs. Youngston nodded, a stubborn set to her jaw. "Do not let your closed mind lead your heart."

"My mind is not closed. I am simply more aware of Dominic's tactics."

Mrs. Youngston bowed her head in disappointment. Knowing she had hurt the woman who'd generously given her a home and a fulfilling role as a teacher, Victoria almost called back her words. Before she could, Mrs. Youngston replied, "I can see you've convinced yourself that Dominic is heartless. The truth is, he needs you. If you look closely, you will see that."

"I looked closely once and he hurt me. Never again," Victoria insisted, denying the hope that tempted her heart to believe the other woman's words.

"Since I cannot force you to look into your heart, perhaps Dominic will persuade you."

"I've already told you, I will not see him."

Mrs. Youngston faced her with a bleak smile. "I fear he's left you no choice. Look behind you."

Fifteen

As Mrs. Youngston's words sank in, Victoria froze. Apprehension flooded her veins, stunning her from action. He was at Pembridge? Now?

Suddenly, a deluge of familiar vibration pervaded her every nerve. She knew Dominic stood mere feet away. Dear God, how could his presence still send wave after tingling wave of sensation through her?

Unbidden, a score of memories rose to the surface—Dominic rising above her in passion, tending the burns to her hands. Pushing her thoughts away, she forced herself to take several deep breaths before she turned to face him.

Across the courtyard, Dominic, indeed, stood, his broad shoulders dominating the frame of Mrs. Youngston's doorway.

Her eyes traveled his length, taking in every nuance, each detail. He had changed. A dark, close-cropped beard now accentuated his square jaw, lending him the ruthless look of a pirate. His raven hair fell almost to his shoulders, adding to his life-at-sea image. The span of his chest, the breadth of his shoulders, seemed broader, more formidable, even beneath the dark wool cloak they filled. His long legs were hard and evocative, conjuring up more memories of their past, their intimacies. She swallowed, wanting so desperately to forget.

His hazel eyes, riveted on her alone, struck her with a new surge of awareness as he stepped into the courtyard.

"Hello, Victoria."

His voice was a mere murmur, but it galvanized her into action with all the ferocity of a roar. Determined to show him—and her heart—that she would no longer dance to his tune, she lifted her skirts and marched straight to him.

Spine ramrod straight, she stood before him. He loomed above her like the archangel Lucifer, his height and breadth intimidating even without the aura of danger that charged at her in waves. But never, Victoria swore, would he dwarf her determination to oust him from her pleasant, albeit safe, life.

He met her stare with a questioning one of his own, his brows drawn together over the eyes still mysterious enough to hide thoughts and feelings . . . yet beautiful enough to draw her into their snare.

His gaze roved unabashedly over her face. Moments later, his thorough inspection traveled down her body. Victoria felt an involuntary tremble. Her blood sluiced hot and liquid as each glance grazed her as tangibly as a physical touch.

Unnerved, she snapped, "Why are you here?"

"Things have gone terribly wrong," he said finally. "You must leave here with me immediately."

It was just as she'd feared; Dominic intended on ripping apart her newfound life. And she would be damned if she were going to let him.

"No, you must leave here immediately—alone." She

stressed every syllable with fury. "You're not wanted here, not by me."

She barely saw the checked fury tighten his face before she turned away and marched back to her room.

Dominic started forward, but Mrs. Youngston held his arm. He heeded the woman's silent advice, then whirled away with a curse, clenching his fists at his sides.

All those months apart had changed nothing. His heart pounded against his ribs, his shaft stood heavy and aching—and she had, as always, caused both reactions. Her contempt, her scorn, while deserved, intensified the ache in his chest. God, how hard he'd fought the dangerous need to hold her, assure her he meant only to protect her.

"Seeing you was a shock for Victoria," Mrs. Youngston counseled.

Dominic sighed. "I had hoped this would not be difficult."

"Perhaps you can persuade her to discuss your plans tomorrow," Mrs. Youngston suggested.

"Not perhaps. I must persuade her. Time is running out. Phillip and his mongrels are not far behind me."

"Be cautious how you approach her."

"The time for caution is past. I will bloody well get her to safety before Phillip arrives, even if I have to drag her every mile of the way."

"Are you concerned Dalmont will wed Victoria and win this foolish game of revenge?"

Dominic shook his head, his mood tense, somber. "I begin to think there can be no winner, except hate."

Mrs. Youngston regarded Dominic as he gazed into the still, white distance. "So you still love her?"

He dipped his head, contemplating the telling question. Love? The sight of her across the courtyard, all wide indigo eyes and soft, never-to-be-forgotten curves, had impacted his gut like a blow, suspending his breath, ripping desire through his body. "Why do you ask?"

"I cannot, in good conscience, release her to you if you plan to seduce her again. And since men in love will do unpredictable things . . ."

"You may rest your fears. Whatever I once felt for her is properly buried," he gritted out between clenched teeth.

"Splendid, since the same can be said for her feelings."

Naturally. A woman's "love" never lasted long. Why had he hoped differently?

Dominic shook his head, refusing to think about it. "Good. Then there will be no possibility of romantic entanglements."

"Oh, no. She told me not long ago she would rather devote her life to God," Mrs. Youngston said, smoothing her skirts.

Pride boosted Dominic's anger. So she professed to prefer chastity, did she? Perhaps he should show her differently.

No, he could not, he remembered moments later. Whenever he touched her, inevitably he emerged from the encounter both shaken and burned. He refused to repeat the pain.

Mrs. Youngston offered, "Supper should be served in no more than an hour. I could arrange for you to dine with Victoria in the kitchen."

Dominic hesitated, debating on the wisdom of such

seclusion. *This time it will be different,* he vowed. *This time I will resist her allure, no matter what.*

That decided, he replied, "Please do."

Victoria did not appear for supper.

As Mary approached him the following morning, wincing, Dominic knew the meek woman would give him news he would not like.

She cleared her throat delicately.

Dominic speared her with a sharp glance. "What is it?"

"Victoria simply will not leave her chamber."

"She must eat sometime."

Mary bowed her head. "I believe she said she would prefer starvation to your company."

Dominic clenched his napkin in his fist, striving to cool his anger. When he had been told she could not be persuaded to leave her quarters the past evening, he had prayed this morning would be soon enough to warn her. But her latest slur was more than he could bear, to know that she preferred both chastity and starvation to a few minutes with him.

"Did she say anything else?" he asked tightly.

Wide-eyed, the girl opened her mouth then quickly closed it. "I should not repeat it."

"I need to know," he growled.

She hesitated. "She said she wished very much that you would rot in . . . hell."

With a terse jerk of frustration, Dominic threw his head back. He stared at the ceiling and strove for patience, only to find fear and urgency had replaced that quality this morning.

"Shall I deliver a message to her?" the teacher asked.

Dominic stood and threw his napkin on the table. "No, thank you. I will tell her myself."

He stalked up the stairs, toward the east wing teachers' quarters. His long, angry strides echoed through the dark, tiled hallways in cadence with the blood pounding in his ears. He would wring her neck until she listened, if he could just get his hands around her lovely little throat.

When he reached her door, he sucked in a calming breath and knocked.

"Who is it?" Victoria inquired cautiously.

Satisfied that she had no escape, Dominic tried to turn the knob. His ire rose a notch higher when he found it locked.

"Victoria, open the bloody door!"

"Not for you."

"I need to talk to you. Open it," he demanded.

"I will do no such thing."

"If you don't open the door, I will break it down."

"Your growling no longer scares me. After all, you've done your worst," she added acidly.

"If you're no longer frightened, then you will come out and talk to me," he countered.

She hesitated a beat, then replied, "It's hardly fear that keeps me from facing you. I simply have nothing to say except *goodbye.*"

"Damn it, Victoria. Listen to me, just for a few minutes."

Silence.

Dominic paused to lean against the portal separating them. He groped for the words to convince her she must listen. "I know you hate me," he began, "but this is too important to ignore. I'm talking about your *life.*"

Victoria hesitated. "I will meet you in the courtyard in five minutes."

Dominic entered the dormant, well-kept garden via a side entrance. From a distance, he studied Victoria's delicate profile as she sat upon the bench, enveloped in a cloak that seemed to match the deep shade of her blue eyes.

He sighed in deep thought. Victoria *was* different now; confidence echoed in her voice and gave her chin a prideful lift. Self-assurance fit her like a perfectly tailored garment, adding another fascinating dimension to the woman he'd tried so hard to banish from his thoughts.

As he stepped toward her, Dominic knew the instant she became aware of his presence; she froze in mid-motion. Stiffly, she turned and met his gaze.

By a sweep of his hand, Dominic asked silently if he could sit beside her. She paused a moment before scooting to the edge of the bench. Without a word, he sat.

The chilly breeze drifted in his direction, carrying a trace of her scent. Instantly, it evoked an image of her as they had last made love, urgently on his bed—her thin chemise clinging to the soft curves of her body; her dark, damp hair curling around her shoulders, soft against the skin of his chest as she bent to kiss him . . .

"What do you want?" she asked coolly, interrupting his runaway memory.

He breathed deeply, admonishing himself for the remembrance. "You wrote a letter to your father since I left you."

Victoria sent him a defiant glance. "Indeed. Three months past."

"I told you not to," he bit out before he could stop himself.

"I have no need to listen to you anymore." She stood and began to make her way inside.

Dominic reached inside her cloak and grabbed her arm, pulling her back to his side. Having her warm skin beneath his fingers for the first time in six months made him ache with instant desire.

He pushed the sensation aside. "Listen to me!"

She jerked her arm from his grasp. "I don't have to do anything not of my choosing. And I would think that, if for no other reason than that you used me in the most despicable way possible, you would have the decency to leave me in peace."

He curled his hands into fists, trying to block out the urge to feel her passionate mouth against his. "And because you chose not to heed my advice, because you told your father you were safely at an orphanage, he shared that letter with Phillip."

"I did not indicate the name or location of Pembridge."

"That hardly matters, damn it. I had Phillip believing I killed you so he would leave you alone."

Shock zipped across her face. "I will not believe such drivel. Even if I did, you are the last person I would go anywhere with."

"Drivel? Surely you noticed a dress missing from your valise after I departed."

Wearing a confused frown, she nodded.

"I took it, found a farmer slaughtering his pig, and dipped it in the animal's blood. I sent the dress, with my knife, to Phillip. He called off the searches."

Victoria scowled. "That is insanity."

"It worked," he growled, "until you wrote that

bloody letter. How many orphanages do you think Phillip would associate with me? Only the one where I grew up. So he and his men will arrive soon, probably within a day. You know he is capable of the worst, Victoria."

"What can Dalmont do to me now? He has no reason to hurt me."

Dominic grasped her shoulders, willing her to understand while willing his own desire away. "Victoria, you don't know Phillip as I do. There is no limit to his cruelty when crossed. Make no mistake, he still wants you and might well bind you to him for a lifetime, then spend every day of it hurting you."

She shook off his touch. "I will take that risk."

Dominic drew in a long breath, mentally regaining control of his temper. "Leave with me quietly." When she opened her mouth to protest, he cut in. "I'm giving you the option of walking out the door on your own, thus allowing you to say farewell to everyone, or of being carried out."

"Damn you. Why act as if you care what happens to the lowly pawn you made your whore?"

His fingers curled around her wrist, unyielding. "I *never* thought of you in that way. I—" Dominic stopped, knowing to say any more of his feelings was dangerous for both of them. He released her. "I do not want to see you endure Phillip's cruelty."

"And what safe haven do you propose to send me to now?" she asked, placing her hands on her hips in a pose of defiance. "Another remote cottage where you can lure me to your bed?"

Guilt and fury each took a part of his heart and pulled. "France," he bit out. "We'll journey to London. I have a friend there who owns a shipping business. Randall will cross the channel to Calais with you, where you will disembark. From there, he will see you safely to Paris and into hiding."

"And where will you go?"

"Not to Paris, if that is what you ask."

Chin set, she shook her head, wisps of copper curls brushing her neck. "I cannot abandon these children. They need me. That is far more important than Dalmont's plot or your wishes."

Willing her to understand, he grabbed her hands. "I doubt Phillip is above harming children to get what he wants. Do you want to risk their safety simply to prove your anger to me?"

She gasped, eyes wide with fury. "You snake!"

"Thank you for that opinion," he said, trying to appear unaffected. "Now, will you come with me quietly?"

The bottomless blue eyes he remembered so well cast him an accusing glare. "As usual, you leave me with virtually no choice. But do not think for an instant I will allow you to touch me."

"I would not dream of laying a hand on your . . . person, my lady. Meet me out front in an hour."

With that, he spun away and left the garden, wondering how the hell he was going to keep his hands off her on the long journey to London.

Sixteen

Scarcely an hour later, Victoria met Dominic in front of Pembridge. As he strapped their belongings onto the two horses, she said her goodbyes.

Mary hugged Victoria quickly, then departed before the burst of tears fell from her usually placid eyes.

Mrs. Youngston coddled Mary, then urged the other teacher back inside. Victoria watched her friend walk away, fighting the tears tightening her throat.

Next, Victoria bid farewell to three young girls. She gave each a drawing of themselves, along with a shaky smile.

The girls clung to her. "We shall miss you, Miss Tory."

"As I shall miss you. All of you."

She knelt, clasping each student against her. Their warm bodies and hot tears covered her. Her heart ached, heavy and desolate. How could she leave children who had known so little love in their lives? Yet she knew she must. For their safety, she would endure this journey and upheaval in her life, all courtesy of Dominic.

He stood behind her. She glared over her shoulder at him as she released the girls and rose to her feet.

Face pensive, he turned away and strode to check the horses.

Mrs. Youngston approached. "Back to the house, girls. Supper awaits."

With downcast faces and downtrodden gaits, they went inside, waving small fingers. Victoria's heart wrenched again.

"I know you and Dominic have had some difficult times," Mrs. Youngston whispered a moment later, urging her farther away from Dominic. "But he cares for you. Do try to forgive him."

Knowing that to refute her claim of Dominic's feeling would only earn her further argument, she said, "As soon as I am able, I shall return and resume teaching."

Surprise filtered across Mrs. Youngston aging face. "No. Your time with us is over."

"Don't you want me to resume the childrens' studies?"

The older woman regarded her with an expression of motherly concern. "If I thought such would truly make you happy, then yes. But you will never be truly happy here, merely content."

Victoria frowned, puzzled. "Are they not the same?"

"Oh, not at all. When I ran from my love and hid here, I felt safe. Now that he is gone, I regret my decision. I was not brave enough to face him or the truth. I was lulled by tranquility but never knew rapture. Do not repeat my mistake."

Just then, Callie ran to Victoria and clung to her skirt. Victoria lifted the toddler in her arms, trying hard not to show the tears she resented Dominic and Dalmont both for causing.

"Don't go," the girl insisted.

The tears finally spilled in searing droplets down Victoria's cheeks, chilled by the winter wind. "I have to, pumpkin. But I will think of you each day."

Mrs. Youngston hugged the crying child and took her away. When the door closed behind them, despair rolled through her. Victoria felt as if part of her life had ended irrevocably. Then she chastised herself for such frivolity. She would come back.

All at once, she became aware of Dominic's scrutinizing stare. She met it measure for measure, refusing to blink.

"We'll ride until sunrise, maybe longer," he said finally.

She shrugged. "Whatever you wish. My only concern is in reaching London quickly."

"So you can be rid of me?"

"Did you expect differently?"

"Not at all," he answered tightly.

Victoria saw his broad shoulders stiffen before he turned away and set his horse at a trot.

The moon is a mysterious thing, Victoria decided two nights later as she snuggled deep beneath her blankets on the hard winter ground and stared up. The hazy, golden sliver of an orb hung low in the sky, lying lazily on its back. Only days ago, its color had been bright and revealing, its shape full. Now it appeared a mere fraction of itself, its unusual topaz color obscured by fog. It was a chameleon, as life was, ever-changing, and not always for the best.

Her thoughts wandered back to Dominic, as they had constantly since their departure from the orphanage. A secret part of her warmed to the fact Dominic had come, risking his own life to protect her. Though why her safety concerned him now remained a puzzle.

Shaking her head at her own foolishness, she looked away from the hypnotic shade of the moon. Dominic had seduced and left her, then forced her to abandon a fulfilling role as teacher—all because he had demanded revenge and used her to achieve it. She should not be so thin-headed as to consider his misdeeds in any other light.

The crunch of boots on dark, dry earth resonated about the fireless camp. The cadence of the walk and the matching vibration within told Victoria that Dominic stood behind her. Dread mixed with a dangerous spark of anticipation.

She sat up and twisted around to meet his gaze. "What do you want?"

He paced to her side, then set his foot on a fallen log beside her. She cast a cautious glance up as he leaned forward, resting his arm on bent knee.

He looked touchable, with a disturbing hint of little-boy-lost on his bearded countenance. Yet those long legs, encased in snug black breeches, reminded her of the pleasure only a man could give.

Dragging her gaze back to his face, she watched his inky hair ruffle in the night's breeze, noticed that his eyes shone in an intriguing green-gold mix, even in the moon's muted light.

Ignoring a sudden whirl in her stomach, Victoria clasped her shaking hands together in her lap. "I asked you what you want."

Dominic leaned closer, until their faces were inches apart. "You did not eat supper again. I worried you might be ill."

He was too close. Desperately, she wanted to retreat, but refused to reveal how thoroughly his proximity disturbed her.

She pushed aside the nervous bite in her stomach.

"In order to worry, Dominic, a person must care, which you do not. If nothing else, do not lie to me."

He seized her wrist, dragging her into the circle of his heat, into the very contact she wanted to deny. "I have never lied to you. Never."

Releasing her suddenly, as if her touch stung him, Dominic stepped back. Victoria let out a silent sigh of relief.

"If you are not ill, why didn't you eat?" he probed.

"I have no desire to share your company."

"You cannot continue to avoid every meal just to avoid me."

Her chin rose a notch. "If I choose to, that is my right."

He leaned forward, seizing her arms and pulling her close. "You will need your strength for this journey. Phillip's men are not far behind. We cannot risk your taking ill from weakness."

"What is this farce, the act of the concerned swain?"

As he pulled her yet closer, his fingers tightened around her, gripping the flesh of her upper arms. "I have always been concerned for you, Victoria."

His voice caressed her, velvety soft. It held a subtle suggestion of tenderness she felt sure he hadn't intended.

A moment later his scent reached her, something so unique to him she had ceased trying to define the source, not just rich soil or coffee or thunderous rain. Whatever its combination, it washed over her senses. She reached out, praying for the strength to push him away.

Dominic paused, his gaze straying down to where she touched his chest. Then his stare rose to her face again, his hazel eyes holding her prisoner. Instantly, she felt something leap between them, an emotion both familiar and treacherous, curling around her heart until it raced.

In denial, she tore her hand away, then retreated to her blankets. "Your concern comes too late. Leave me be, Dominic."

At sundown on the eighth day of their arduous journey, Dominic and Victoria approached a dirt-streeted village. Victoria wanted to be curious about the first glimpse of civilization she'd had since leaving the orphanage, but was too tired. Her abused backside felt further bruised with each of her mount's steps. Despite the wide-brimmed hat Dominic insisted she wear, all-day exposure to the sun left her weak.

But she found the discomfort of her body easier to bear than the memories she dared not voice—memories that filled her thoughts during their silent, seemingly eternal journey. And questions plagued her, too. Did Dominic care, as he had suggested nearly a week ago? She sighed as memory, emotion, and uncertainty coalesced within her.

Her gaze strayed to Dominic, sitting atop his gray. He held the reins loosely, his long fingers at ease with the leather.

Those hands were capable of giving such pleasure, of making her feel so cherished. If he touched her tonight and whispered sweetly of his ardor, would she be able to resist him?

Suddenly, Dominic met her stare with an inquiring brow raised. Hating the guilty blush burning across her cheeks, she glanced away.

"You shouldn't look at me like that, my lady," he warned.

"Like what?" She feigned innocence, sizzling inside.

He turned those stunning hazel eyes on her. She steeled herself for his mocking glint, but froze in surprise when their gazes met. His taut-jawed face held the look of rampant emotions barely in check. With blazing, almost pleading eyes, he stared, motionless. That look sent a bolt of fear all the way to the pit of her stomach.

Finally, he tore his gaze away to stare out at the small-town scenery. "Perhaps we should discuss your thoughts."

Fighting the urge to panic, she shook her head and hid behind sarcasm. "So you want to discuss what an ogre you are?"

"Victoria . . ." His sigh was long, slow, and resigned. "I realize I hurt you, damn it. But I can clearly see you have not forgotten us anymore than I have."

She shot him a scathing glare. "You see nothing."

His reckless gaze held a challenge of its own. "Nothing? Your liquid eyes and flushed cheeks, parted lips and dreamy expression are an exact mirror of your face when we made love."

"My eyes are liquid from the dust, my cheeks flushed from exhaustion. If my lips are parted, it is because I desire nothing more than a drink of cool water. And you misread a bored expression as a dreamy one."

Swallowing nervously, Victoria cast her gaze to Dominic. His dubious stare told her he disbelieved her impassioned speech. Perdition, why couldn't she fool him this once?

Beneath his beard, Dominic's jaw tightened. His narrowed eyes accented a severe frown. "Why deny the truth?"

Not knowing what else to say, she nudged her mare

ahead, dodging his damning stare. Her whole body
shook. Dominic's eyes raked her back, burning her
skin. She didn't want to talk about her desires. Even if
Dominic were ready now to give his love freely, she had
no intention of allowing him close enough to hurt her
again. She was through taking risks with her heart.

Victoria rounded the corner of a crumbling stone
church. Her eyes widened in alarm when she spotted
four uniformed men, all sporting the Dalmont crest
upon their chest.

Fear pumped through her veins as she halted her
horse.

"Stop!" she hissed, surveying the men's actions.

"A search party?" Dominic asked behind her.

She nodded almost imperceptibly.

"They have not seen me as yet. I can overtake them."

"Too many," she whispered.

"I do not want you in danger. We will outrun them."

She bowed her head and pretended to adjust her hat.
"They have already seen me. Running would give us
away. You must hide."

He paused. "What will you do?"

She lifted her shoulders a fraction in a shrug.

"Try to rid yourself of them. I will be watching," he
vowed.

Victoria nodded, then listened as Dominic, obviously
reluctant, turned his horse toward the abandoned mon-
astery. Nudging her mare a few steps forward, she
hoped Dominic would have enough time to hide well.

"Miss, are you alone?" the man who was clearly their
leader inquired, stepping toward her. He sounded per-
plexed.

"Yes, I seem to be lost." She cursed the slight quiver
in her voice.

The young man, short and mustached, continued to eye her. "And what is your name, pray tell?"

She paused, searching her racing mind for anything plausible. "Miss Charlotte Little."

At that, the man guffawed. Another whispered something in his ear. They turned and stared at her breasts, laughing uproariously.

The young leader turned lascivious eyes on her. "My friend noticed that your name doesn't quite describe your anatomy, Miss . . . Little."

Indignation filled her belly with a hot rage—until his words gave her an idea. She stifled her anger and smiled.

"You can only imagine," she whispered huskily.

Taking a step forward, he grabbed her reins. "Truly?"

Victoria untied the chin strap of her straw hat and removed it, allowing her red curls to tumble down her back and around her shoulders. She shook her head for effect. "Truly."

"I should like to do more than imagine."

The man slid his hand up her thigh, and Victoria hid her fist beneath the folds of her dress, wishing she could let it fly into his arrogant face.

She forced herself to smile. "Come with me, and you shall."

"I cannot leave my post, sweet."

"Would you not rather be with me?" She pretended a pretty pout.

"I can come to you later," he suggested. "Tonight."

Victoria shook her head. "I will most certainly have changed my mind by then." She leaned closer and whispered, "I need you now."

The young leader paused, then shook his head. Victoria fought rising panic.

"Perhaps he ain't capable, eh?" one of the other men chortled. "Maybe, blokes, he don't know how."

"Aye," another red-faced man answered, barely suppressing a laugh. "Maybe he's afraid she'll hurt 'im."

The young leader turned an angry glare to his chuckling companions, then looked back at Victoria. "Let's go."

The other men slapped him on the back and, with a wink in Victoria's direction, sauntered back down the road and disappeared. Victoria held in her sigh of relief. She had successfully narrowed down the odds to something more favorable. She and Dominic could best this popinjay.

Then the man grasped Victoria's wrist and pulled. She fell off her mount, against his chest. With intense black eyes, he glared down into her face. "I am Colin, and I promise you will not forget me."

His expression, somewhere between resentment and lust, prickled Victoria with anxiety. What if success weren't as easily won as she'd thought?

Colin's lips descended on hers, crushing, bruising. Victoria stumbled back with the force. Fighting down rising panic, she realized he was backing her in Dominic's direction.

She threw her arms around Colin's shoulders in feigned passion. The skin beneath his uniform was damp with sweat, despite the winter breeze. His mouth opened above hers a moment before his tongue invaded. She fought the urge to bite down. Instead, she continued to draw him toward the church, inch by tension-filled inch.

Victoria felt Colin's hands searching, grasping for the

buttons at the back of her dress. When he discovered them, he grabbed the first, ripping it from its hole. Victoria maneuvered herself against the old building's gray wall and, fighting her rising apprehension, prayed Dominic would come to her aid soon.

Colin stiffened then. Victoria looked up and found Dominic's hand pulling the other man's hair, his knife at the astonished guard's throat. His expression seethed with fury.

"Take your hands off her," Dominic commanded.

"She invited me to kiss her. I swear," Colin babbled.

"She lied." His voice was as unbendable as steel. "Release her."

Colin's hands left her. Cautiously, he raised them above his head as Dominic instructed.

"Good. Step away, my lady."

Victoria did so, sucking in a breath of relief.

Using the butt of his knife, Dominic struck the other man's head. Colin slumped back, and Dominic dragged the unconscious man into the shade of the church's alcove.

When Dominic returned, he grabbed Victoria's shoulders and, without a word, refastened the buttons Colin had not torn off. He shot her a harsh glare before mounting his horse and motioning her to follow.

"The sun is nearly down," Dominic said suddenly. "We will stop here for now. London is a few hours away yet, but we will wait until after midnight to enter the city."

With a shaky nod, Victoria dismounted to the soft earth between a pair of trees. She said nothing, not trusting her voice. The abduction, the torment on her heart, her time with Dominic . . . all of it would end in mere hours. She should be happy.

Happiness had never made her ache so deeply.

She turned away until Dominic handed her their foodstuffs.

Exhaustion seeped into Victoria's every pore as she ate the dried beef and drank water. She wanted her blankets and a good night's sleep.

And to forget this would be her last night with Dominic.

Pushing the thought away, she set the remnants of her meal aside and made to rise. Her wobbling legs, weak from so many hours in the saddle, protested. She grasped about, looking for something solid with which to regain her balance. Dominic stood behind her an instant later, clasping her hand in his and leaning her against the breadth of his chest. Warm breath tickled her ear.

Victoria's pulse leapt at the contact. His palm burned against hers as he entwined their fingers in an unbearably intimate gesture. His hands lingered on her waist, fingers drawing breathlessly close to her breasts. A fiery spark danced within her belly as she inhaled his scent. Why did the awareness, the want, still storm between them now that she needed to forget him?

She eased away from him, body stiff. "Thank you."

Dominic regarded her, his head cocked. "No, I should thank you. After all, you saved my life today."

"I merely kept your presence a secret."

He grabbed her arm. "At the risk of your own safety. Why?"

Panic assailed her as she felt the dangerous heat of his fingers. She tried twisting from his grasp. "Let me go."

"Tell me why, my lady. You could have let me die. You would have been rid of me forever."

His hazel eyes probed to her soul. That gaze told her he wanted to touch her. His taut countenance conveyed desire with frightening clarity—and something more. Pain? Yes, it was pain. She had the strangest urge to comfort him, even though she feared he would sweep her into the tidal wave of his need—and she would lose her heart again.

"I am truly sorry," he whispered suddenly. "For everything. I am not proud of what I've done."

She swallowed, nodding tightly, uncertain whether to rail at him or cry.

"Victoria, we have less than twelve hours left together, damn it. Say something."

Victoria's gaze snapped to his. *Less than twelve hours?*

Her gaze roved over his strong face, across the rugged planes of his cheeks, focusing on his knowing eyes. Memories, so few, yet cherished, rushed back to her. Faced with their parting, her heart finally admitted what her pride had tried so hard to deny: She still cared for him.

Drawing in a deep breath, Victoria raised her gaze from the Spartan winter growth around her feet to his oh-so-familiar face.

"We should spend our last hours together wisely." Her voice sounded raspy in the thick air.

A wary question flashed across Dominic's face. "Wisely?"

"You are leaving me again. And this time, as last, I've no choice." She stared, willing him to understand. "Touch me once more. Just once."

He backed away from her. "Victoria—"

"You still want me. Admit it." She took a step closer.

"I admit it freely. But it changes nothing."

"Do not leave me forever without touching me one last time."

Her gaze locked with his. His green-gold eyes penetrated her upturned face. Resistance faded from his features, replaced by the hungry expression that had haunted her during her long nights at Pembridge. Yet unlike those black, empty hours, she welcomed the searing awareness that shocked her with want.

He curled his hands into fists and bowed his head. After a reluctant sigh, he lifted his tormented gaze to her. "God help me, I cannot turn you away any more than I can stop breathing."

Dominic reached for her, grasping the back of her head, tangling his fingers in her curls. Slowly, he drew her against him. Trapped by his gaze, Victoria watched as his expression became a dark vortex of desire so compelling, she found herself caught up in it . . . hypnotized by it.

"Having you in my arms, beside me, beneath me, is all I have thought of since we left the orphanage. I want you, more than anything, anyone, I have ever wanted."

His words sent her momentarily tamed pulse into turmoil once again. Joy erupted within her.

"I want you, too," she whispered, trembling.

His mouth descended on hers. Victoria parted her lips to receive his passionate onslaught. His tongue swept past the barrier of her lips, asking for her response.

That kiss, his touch, was everything she remembered—and more. The warm taste of him invaded, then overpowered her senses. His arms tightened around her, drawing her in so closely she felt every inch of his body, including his arousal against her belly. His achingly familiar scent, a heady musk, penetrated her senses in conjunction with the soft caress of his tongue as it again entered her mouth, shattering both of them.

She clutched at his shoulders, seeking his support. He lent it gladly, at the cost of an additional kiss, more enthralling than the last. He lifted his hands to her face, caressing her and guiding her response.

The tumult within her crashed like the ocean against the hard rock of the shore. She moaned into his mouth, treasuring each kiss, memorizing his texture, his scent, his heartbeat against her own.

With a hand supporting her back, he leaned forward, guiding her to the soft forest floor. He raised his hand to her face and, with his thumb, skimmed her bottom lip. His gaze never left her face, as if he were trying to memorize her.

Dominic's fingers fell to the tiny buttons down the front of her dress. Deftly, he undid the first few and folded the fabric down to give his mouth access to the soft flesh of her breast and the delicacy of its crowning crest.

He nibbled the sweet bud of that mound, tasting it, groaning all the while. The sound of his desire vibrated through her, intensifying the ache he created with the finesse of an artist.

The sensual persuasion of his mouth coaxed her to arch against him. She felt his hand on her thigh, reaching up higher, lifting her chemise, caressing her hip. The warm texture of his palm lingered against the skin of her inner thigh, the rough tips of his fingers climbing toward the apex. She ached for his hand there, wanted it—wanted him.

He insinuated his leg between hers and began nibbling on her neck, whispering the erotic promises she had craved for six isolated months.

His teeth nipped at the underside of her chin. She felt the heat of his other palm scorch the taut flesh of her breast. His tongue touched her abdomen, and she found herself hoping feverishly his mouth would climb just a little higher.

As if he read her mind, he took the tight bud of her breast in his mouth again. Her arms flew around his shoulders as her fingers tangled in the hair at his nape. Oh, how she remembered him, every little detail, the clean scent of his ebony hair, the musky smell of his skin. She stored the impressions away in memory.

Desire swelled and throbbed within her as he looked at her once more. Her gaze took in the glint of his hazel eyes, the raw need in his expression.

Dominic's hands flew to the buttons of his breeches in the next instant. Victoria listened as he ripped them in haste. Her anticipation climbed. He pushed and tugged until his breeches gathered around his hips, freeing his arousal.

Moving on top of her, he murmured, "Open for me."

Reading the want in his eyes that mirrored her own, she did.

With one solid push, he thrust into her.

"Victoria." His low, reverent rasp feathered across her senses, dissipating both doubts and logic.

He drew away, almost to the point of withdrawal, then pressed into her once more. This time, he went deeper, igniting all her sensations. She loved the feel of him, the taste of him.

She loved him.

Dominic established a rhythm, immersing himself inside her over and over with deep strokes. She cried out as the need within her coiled into a tight spring, aching for release.

His movements became faster still, this time more overwhelming than she could fight. Swiftly, her arousal rose to new, almost frightening heights. Her heart leapt at their togetherness, the need they had created. The edge of pleasure rushed up to her and she tumbled over.

The riotous colors of his stunning hazel eyes exploded in her mind as ecstasy washed over her with amazing ferocity. She clutched his shoulders, paralyzed by pleasure. A moment later, he surrendered to satisfaction with a groan.

Slowly, their movements came to a halt. Dominic lay still above her, even as silence seized the woods around them. Her breathing slowed. The enormity of what had happened loomed in the quiet, crashing into Victoria's heart with the violent, unrelenting return of doubts and fears.

Dominic lifted his head to study her. Victoria's face was a banquet of eloquent expressions—exultation, uncertainty . . . and remorse. She'd wanted him, true, but nothing had changed. He had nothing to give her.

Damn, but he'd been a bloody fool to succumb to his urge to touch her, to the love he could not hold back anymore. Not that he was surprised, for she always affected him so. He had ached to touch Victoria, just once more. Experience had warned him he was playing with fire. He'd gotten too close—and she had burned him again, leaving his heart in ashes.

He closed his eyes, feeling the tremors of pain twisting at his gut . . . and soul. But he did not blame her for hating him. How could he when the fault rested so squarely on his shoulders? He'd put her through a harrowing ordeal. And passion, no matter how perfect, would never change her resentment. Nor could his love, no matter how deep, erase the fact that, for her safety, they had to part. Tonight.

"I will leave so you can dress in privacy," he offered finally, rising to his feet and adjusting his clothing.

"Yes, please." Her voice hung between them, strained and tight, as she covered herself and looked away.

Swallowing everything else he wanted to say, Dominic walked away.

In the forest's predawn dark, Dominic awakened Victoria. They readied for the last part of their journey in silence, the night's chill no less cool than the air between them.

Victoria wished Dominic would say something, acknowledge what had happened between them, but knew he would not.

After a wordless preparation and cold breakfast, he helped her mount before he did the same and set his gray to a trot.

Despite her bruised backside, the ride passed too quickly. She wondered what he would do after he left her—continue to run from Dalmont or flee the country? Victoria knew he would not care, but she would pray each night for his safety.

Minutes after reaching London Harbour, Dominic grabbed her reins, stopping her horse before a warehouse.

"See that, my lady?" he said, pointing to a tall, two-masted vessel at anchor. At her hesitant nod, he continued, "That is your ship to safety. It leaves tomorrow morning."

Despair burning within her, Victoria dismounted and darted toward the pier. Soon Dominic was behind her, guiding her onto the ship.

The cloying pungency of the damp salt air did nothing to ease the tension thrumming from him. Soupy fog hung all around, matching her sorrowful mood.

God, how she wanted to cry. He was truly leaving her, forever this time, regardless of what they had shared just hours ago. Though it was foolish, she'd hoped he had felt the love in her embrace. Apparently, he'd felt nothing but lust for her—ever. Victoria tried to tell herself she was lucky to be rid of him.

She cursed both her luck and her logic.

Once on deck, Dominic and the captain exchanged pleasantries. From the hearty handshakes, it was clear they were friends. Drat, she didn't want to go to Paris, not any more than she wanted to leave Dominic. Living in a new city amongst strangers held no appeal. Perhaps going to cousin Henry's to be with her father would soothe her soul and his grief. Family might take away the pain. Someday, she might be able to remember Dominic and not feel the wrenching of her heart.

And the stars might fall from the sky.

All too soon, he escorted her below deck to a small cabin he indicated would be hers for the duration of the journey. He set her satchel in the corner, then withdrew a black velvet pouch from his pocket. It made the clink of gold as he set it on the table.

"This is for you. It should see you to Paris and give you ample funds to live on for some months." He folded the pouch in her palm.

A moment of incredulity held her tongue captive. Money. Did he think to pay her for the use of her body? Assuage his guilt? Fury and hurt blended into a combustive explosion, and she hurled the pouch at him. It landed squarely against his chest, then made a thud as it fell to the wooden floor at his feet. "I will not accept your bloody coin."

He retrieved and set it on the tiny table beside him with a fierce scowl. "You will need it in Paris."

In the powerful silence that followed, Dominic dropped his gold-green gaze from hers and turned away. "When it is safe for you to return to England, I will send word."

"Well, you have thought of everything, haven't you? You've given me money and sent me on my way." Hurt tore through her. She blinked away the tears stinging her eyes. "How pleasant for you to be rid of me so easily."

"You knew from the first we would part. If you expected something more emotional, I'm sorry." He inclined his head forward in a gesture of formal politeness, his face a perfectly blank mask. "Have a safe journey."

Seventeen

Restless and red-eyed, Victoria woke in the ship's cramped bunk hours before dawn, feeling the bob and sway of the vessel anchored at port . . . and the void of Dominic's absence.

Sitting up among the blankets, her gaze shifted listlessly about the small cabin without really seeing her surroundings. The lack of his warmth and touch tore through her heart like a jagged stake. From her stint at Pembridge, she remembered well the reality of awaking without him every morning, of being without him each day. Everything inside her, from her grieving mind to her shattered heart still wanted to cry, to protest that Dominic's departure had stripped away half of her soul.

Though duty prevailed her to eventually try to find a husband, the thought of doing so repulsed her. Dominic lived in her heart and soul, whether he wanted to be there or not. She couldn't imagine allowing another man the intimacies they had shared. She only knew she must tell her father she could not wed Dalmont. He would honor her wishes in that, she was sure.

Victoria found slipping off the ship and onto the docks no problem. As she crept about the rough, foul-smelling walkways, hiring a hackney to take her to a coaching inn proved more difficult.

Determination beat soundly inside her to reach her father and start her life anew. A life without Dominic. Still, she couldn't suppress a shiver from winding up her back at the coarse dockside passersby and the eerie fog.

Cautiously, she made her way past the decrepit shanties lining the deserted, East End streets—and their seedy inhabitants.

Without warning, a large hand reached from behind her, looming above her face before its sweaty palm closed over her mouth.

Panic migrated from all regions of her body and converged in her chest. Another pair of hands grabbed her wrists, and though she struggled, the men's superior strength held her until they'd bound her arms behind her back. She tried to scream for help, but one of the men stuffed a rag in her mouth, silencing her.

"Keep quiet, ye slut," growled one thug in a slum-roughened voice. He lifted her, and Victoria caught a glimpse of a greasy, unwashed hunk of a man, his narrow face pockmarked and cruel, before he threw her in the back of a waiting carriage and followed her in.

She squirmed for freedom as they crossed town and tried to work at the binds of her wrists. She kicked the fiend restraining her. He simply took her legs into his hands and fondled her calves, laughing at her discomfort and ire. The other cull grinned wickedly over his shoulder as he drove.

Repeatedly, she prayed Dalmont wasn't behind this scheme. Sweet mercy, if he were . . . She heard Dominic's words of warning echoing in her head, *He is dangerous.*

She felt no surprise, only skin-tingling fear, when Dalmont's town house came into view.

The burly, rough-faced men pushed her out of the carriage. Victoria scarcely landed on her feet before one prodded her round to the back door. Dread pounded in her heart. What should she say to Dalmont?

One of Victoria's abductors opened the door and pushed her into the warmth of the deserted kitchen. Her wrists still bound behind her, they guided her with hard, grasping hands through the foyer, past the gallery, and into a drawing room.

Before her, Dalmont slouched in a velvet chair of demonic red, looking like the filthy ruler of Hell. His straight flaxen hair hung limply about his face. His blue eyes were watery and bloodshot, perfectly matching the hole in his hose, the scuffs on his shoes, and the stains on his neckcloth.

At first sight of her, Phillip's eyes bulged with shock. He leapt from his chair and grabbed her arm, jerking her closer. Turning, he demanded of the two men, "Where did you find her?"

"Wandering Seven Dials, guv," one answered.

"How did you reach London?" Dalmont barked at her.

One of the men ripped the vile gag from her mouth. She swallowed a lump of bile rising in her throat and vowed to grovel and lie to the best of her ability. Her future was at stake.

"Dominic released me," Victoria announced, her tone carefully blank.

Despite her fear, the realization that she would, indeed, never see Dominic again stung her eyes with tears.

Dalmont let her arm go and stepped back, scanning her face with speculation. "Are you a virgin any longer?"

Victoria swallowed hard. Her first impulse was to lie,

but she feared he would test that answer personally. Instead, she lowered her face and cried, "He . . . took me to avenge somebody named Marcella, for which I shall always hate him."

"I cannot marry you now, but then Dominic knew that." His voice icy, Phillip inquired, "And did you occupy his bed more than once?"

Victoria hesitated then nodded brokenly, hoping to further discourage any notion of marriage.

His curse was a low hiss. "Willingly, I'll wager. You spread your legs for him and enjoyed it. Corinne always does."

"Corinne? Your maid?" Victoria asked, wide-eyed, cold shock chipping away at her heart.

"Ah, so you were unaware of that." A malicious smile contorted his features.

"It's of no consequence." Pain shafted Victoria's heart as she blurted, "I—I hope they are happy together."

Dalmont scanned her face slowly, thoroughly. She dropped her gaze beneath his scrutiny.

"You whore!" He grabbed her arm, fingers biting cruelly. "Dominic has no stomach for rape. He seduced you, and you, no doubt, loved it."

Victoria recoiled from him, fighting back the urge to hurl insults at him. "That is vulgar!"

"But undoubtedly true," Phillip countered. "Did you hate him even as he pleasured you? Or did that change, as well?"

"I—I hate him still," she answered, cringing at the hesitation in her voice.

"Why don't I believe you?"

"He abducted me against my will and took me to his

bed. How can you think I would love someone like that?"

Dalmont's hand grasped her neck and tightened. Victoria tried to jerk away, but he held fast. White specks whirled in her vision. Fear clawed in her gut.

"You are a very poor liar, Lady Victoria," he said softly, then laughed. "I know you protected him from my search parties mere days ago. You love that worthless knave, and I begin to wonder if he doesn't care for you, as well."

Hiding her surprise at his knowledge, she denied his accusation. "He feels nothing for me."

"We shall see." His hand slid down her arm before he pulled her closer. "He may think he has bested me by taking the virtue of my chosen bride," he whispered menacingly in her ear, "but the war is not over. I will rid myself of him, even if it takes my dying breath. And I think you are the perfect bait to lure him into my trap." Dalmont stared at her with an evil smile. "Yes, I do believe he will come to your rescue."

"Lady Victoria?" the maid Corinne breathed as she crept into the nearly-dark chamber. The woman's eyes scanned her thoroughly. "Are ye well? Unharmed?"

Victoria looked away from Dominic's lover. "I am as well as can be expected."

"And Dominic? Did he get away safely?"

Even the sound of his name on the other woman's lips intensified her pain. "I assume so."

Corinne released a held breath. "I worried. Did Dominic tell ye where 'e planned to travel next?"

Victoria shook her head, hating yet understanding the woman's concern for him. "He said nothing. Where is Dalmont?" she asked, changing the subject.

"With Lord Gaphard and the rest of the men, search
ing for Dominic. But I expect them back soon, Lad
Victoria." Her voice dropped to a whisper, as if the wall
possessed prying ears.

"I've come to help. I have great admiration for the
woman who captured Dominic's heart."

Mouth agape in surprise, Victoria faced the maid
"What makes you think I have done anything of the
sort?"

Corinne's frown was puzzled. "When I saw him last
six months ago, he very nearly admitted his love fo
ye."

Victoria's surprise burst into pure shock. Six month
ago?

"You must be mistaken. That is when he left me."

Corinne shook her head, her smile sad. "I know
Nicky. His words and deeds bespoke his heart clearly."

The maid was lying. She had to be. Victoria glared
at the other woman, afraid to believe anything she said
After all, why would a man leave the lady he loved after
showing contempt for her sentiment?

"I don't believe that. Why would Dominic, your lover
tell you of his feelings for me?"

Seeing the smothered surprise on Corinne's face in
fused her with a moment of triumph. "Nicky *was* me
lover. He refused me when I saw him last because of
his love for ye."

It was Victoria's turn to feel surprise. Shock popped
up within her. Refused her? Dominic had told her of a
woman he had rejected. Corinne, standing with hands
clasped, was that woman.

"Does he know you're here?" the maid asked.

Victoria shook her head "He thinks me in Paris."

She sighed. "That explains Randall's note. Ye were
is missin' passenger."

Nodding, Victoria bit her lip. She hated asking
Dominic's lover, former or not, for a favor. For
Dominic's safety she swallowed her pride. "Do not tell
im I am here. Dalmont will only kill him if he comes."

Corinne paused. "I cannot do that, me lady. Nicky
ould kill me if I failed to tell him. Besides, he deserves
appiness, and I begin to think he will find it with ye."

With a shaky sigh, Dominic sat on the edge of the
unk. For the past two days he had been thankful for
he solace of Randall Foster's ships in harbor. Today,
he small space stifled him, the humid enclosure chok-
ng him—along with his fear.

Images of Victoria screaming for help haunted him.
Regret hounded him as he cursed the nightmarish days
n Newgate where he'd devised and nurtured his plot
or revenge. Seeking his own brand of justice had al-
eady cost Victoria most all she held dear. And Dominic
ad no illusions; before this mad scenario played itself
o the end, it could well cost him his life—and now
erhaps Victoria's, too.

"Do you think he raped her?" he asked Corinne, his
whisper rough and raspy.

She shrugged, giving him no reassurance that Phillip
ad not subjected Victoria to all manner of horrors.

"Yer jaunts across the city, in sight of 'is men, are
ikely keeping Dalmont away from Victoria more than
e planned."

How Dominic hoped that was true. "Damn, this is
ny fault! I should never have left Victoria before Randall's ship departed. Hell, I should never have abducted
Victoria at all."

"Ye can still save her," Corinne said.

"How?" Dominic roared. "Phillip is expecting m
He wants me to charge into his fortress like a wounde
lover. And heaven help me, I want to. I want to mak
him die over and over again for any hurt he's don
her."

Corinne took his hand. "So much in love," she sai
shaking her head. "I never thought to see it."

He wrenched away. "I've done nothing but bring he
pain."

"Hmmm." Corinne shrugged. "I doubt she regre
'er time with ye."

"Who wouldn't regret it while Dalmont ties her u
to do God-knows-what?"

She leaned closer, her eyes consoling. "Ye're too har
on yerself. How could ye have known Dalmont woul
use her as bait to trap you?" she reasoned. "Since y
cannot leave Victoria in 'is clutches, what are we goin
to do?"

"We?" He shot a hard glare to her. "Absolutely no
I will not have you in danger, either."

"That is not yer decision," she reminded him, point
ing a finger in his chest. "Dalmont is expecting ye, no
me. That could work for us."

"I will not take that risk." He sighed heavily. "I mus
accept Phillip's ultimatum."

"Nay!" she protested. "Even if ye allow yerself to b
led like a lamb to the slaughter, ye have no guarante
'e'll let her go. She may go on sufferin' even after ye
death."

Dominic sighed, dropping his forehead into hi
palm, haunted by the remembrance of Victoria's rav
aged expression as he'd conducted his own mock rape

And worse, Dominic knew her pleas and cries wouldn't move Phillip's conscience. The fiend didn't possess one.

"Each time I close my eyes, I hear her screams for my help. Dear God, what if he kills her, as he did Marcella?" He choked, rubbing tense fingers over his eyes to erase the graphic visions. "You're right; I must do something besides surrender. And it must be done right the first time. I won't have a second chance."

"Fire!" a desperate voice called into the dense midnight.

"Fire!" came the call again as the man moved further down the hall, shouting his warning.

Above Victoria's pallet on the floor, Phillip bounded out of bed and struggled to don his breeches with trembling hands.

"Fire?" His voice shook. "Damnation, it's hot in here." Phillip struggled into his shirt. "And getting hotter. I must get out."

He stumbled to the door as smoke entered the room, choking Victoria. Fear pulsed within her like a drumbeat.

"Your Grace," she called. "What about me?"

He never looked her way. "Burn. I don't care. I must escape!"

Dalmont dashed out the door, leaving her tied to the bed's leg. Resisting the urge to panic, she tugged at the ropes about her wrists. Her raw skin bled further in protest.

Terror bubbled inside her. God, she couldn't die here, not like this. She wasn't ready to leave this earth.

Suddenly, the door burst open. A stranger crept in, eyes scanning the room as if searching. Apparently finding nothing, the intruder turned to her in the misty semi-dark and ripped off his mask. Victoria gasped at the sight of Dominic's face.

"Where is Phillip?" he barked.

"Gone."

"Thank God."

He bent to her and clutched her against his chest. A sense of safety enveloped her as he hugged her tightly, his hands moving gingerly up and down her body.

"I am so sorry, my lady." Regret melded his strong features into a frown as he untied the bonds around her wrists. "We must run now, before Phillip discovers the fire is only a small one."

They made their way down the halls, wound through the town house's kitchen, and slipped out a servants' exit into the black, starry night.

Dominic urged her to run once outdoors. Victoria struggled to keep up with him as they darted down Pall Mall, but his stride never slowed. By the time they turned down the Strand, she was seeing stars and her heart felt as if it would beat out of her chest. She leaned forward, gasping for each breath.

"Please, my lady," he urged, curling his arm about her. "Just a little further."

Nodding, Victoria forced her legs to a run once more. Again, he grabbed her hand and pulled her behind him.

Dominic led her down Exchange Street. Victoria now saw the masts of the tall ships above the surrounding buildings as they sprinted to the docks just yards ahead. The damp wood against her bare feet, along with the windy night air, caused her to tremble. No, she realized moments later; fear caused that.

At the edge of the dock, Dominic stooped to cast off a longboat. Anxiously, she looked on in hope.

The thunder of footfall prompted Victoria to look behind her—and her heart to jump into her throat at the sight.

"Give up, Grayson!" Dalmont commanded suddenly, ringed by a dozen of his henchmen.

Dominic glanced at the men before looking back at her. He clasped her hand in his suddenly and squeezed. She knew he planned to jump into the harbor and take her with him.

"Don't try it," Dalmont shouted, obviously having read Dominic's thoughts, too. "Release Victoria's hand.

Dominic hesitated.

"Now!" Dalmont barked. "If you don't, she dies." He pointed a gun to Victoria's chest mere feet away.

Immediately, Dominic moved to release her hand. Victoria tried to clutch her fingers between his.

"No!" she cried, knowing his surrender would mean his death. "Do not give up!"

He appeared not to hear. Slowly, he pulled his fingers from her grasp and raised both hands in the air as a show of surrender.

"What do you want now?" Dominic asked Phillip, his voice tight but toneless.

Dalmont smiled evilly. "I want you to drop to your knees and beg for your life."

"I would rather die," Dominic returned blandly, his face registering both dispassion and contempt.

Displeasure stormed across Phillip's narrow features. He took two steps toward them, and before Victoria could guess his intent, Dalmont grabbed her arm. He jerked, and her back collided with his chest. With an arm around her neck, he pointed his gun to her temple.

"Would you beg for her life?"

Dominic's fists clenched at his sides. "Yes."

Victoria gasped.

"Not a word from you, slut," Dalmont warned, then turned his attention back to Dominic. "If you want her to live, drop to your knees. And beg."

Dominic hesitated not an instant. He dropped to first one knee, then the other. He looked up at Phillip from where he knelt, his face lined and anxious. "Damn you! Keep this hate between *us!* Shoot me, not her."

"I hardly call that begging," Phillip taunted, his demonic smile growing. "But you always were disagreeable."

Dominic closed his eyes with a curse. "What do you want? Blood? Here," he said, thrusting his chest forward in offering. "Take it. All of it. I don't give a damn if you let me bleed to death. Just . . . please . . . do not hurt her."

Again, the evil grin creased Phillip's face. "I've been waiting years to hear you grovel." He nodded in satisfaction. "I will relish the sound always."

Phillip laughed, and Lord Gaphard emerged from the circle. "Seize him!"

A dozen men rushed forward to grab Dominic, and Dalmont released her. Gaphard emerged from the back of the crowd and turned to Phillip. "We should transport him back to Newgate on the morrow."

"No," Phillip insisted. "I told you I wanted Grayson dead. Old Bailey is far too inept to mete out any real justice. Leave that to me."

With those ominous words, the gang of men began to lead Dominic away. Panicked, Victoria tried to grab him, but one of the fiends pushed her.

"Dominic!" she cried as she watched the men kick and drag him forward, away from her.

He turned to look back at her for the brief moment.

Despair and regret etched themselves onto every dark feature of his face, shattering Victoria's heart. Then Phillip's men jerked him forward and forced him away.

"Get her, too," Dalmont commanded.

"Run, Victoria!" shouted Dominic.

Phillip's thugs charged toward her. With a last glance at Dominic's frightened countenance, she jumped into the harbor.

Eighteen

After swimming back to the safety of Randall Foster's ship, Victoria devised a plan. Following the man's directions, Victoria took a hackney to the seedy, East End tavern where Andrew stayed. Her resolve was firm. She would do whatever necessary to make him agree to help her free Dominic.

When she reached the appointed door, Victoria paused to take a nervous breath before she knocked. Would he help? Or refuse her as she had once refused him?

Seconds later, Andrew appeared at the portal, wrinkled shirt askew, his golden hair mussed.

Victoria's first thought was that he looked terribly surprised. Her second was that, other than his disheveled appearance, he had not changed.

After his initial surprise abated, the trembling corners of her mouth tipped up. "Hello, Andrew."

As if suddenly remembering his manners, he stepped back and, with a sweep of his hand, gestured for her to enter.

His room was dark. Tattered, yellowish curtains were drawn over the small, dirty windows. Clothes lay strewn everywhere across the unmade bed. The room's one table was littered with several empty gin bottles and one glass.

"Come in." With his hand, he gestured for her to step further inside. "Excuse the mess. I . . . did not expect company."

"I apologize for this intrusion, but I must speak with you."

"Actually, I was just . . . thinking about you." His blue-gray eyes glowed warmly.

He wasn't angry she had chosen Dominic over him? "Andrew, I did not come to talk about our days at Dominic's cottage."

He nodded, the hunch of his shoulders both contrite and self-deprecating. "I know, but I want to apologize. I suppose Dominic told you what a scoundrel I am, or was anyway. I did see every woman as a conquest. But you *were* different. For the first time, I knew a woman as a person. Victoria, I would have treated you well. I wanted to, but my lust, my jealousy . . ." He paused. "I can only guess the hell he gave you. Again, I apologize." He shut the door behind her and sat, motioning her to join him on the sofa. "Where is my esteemed friend? Did Dominic release you?"

Pain arced through her heart as she sat beside Andrew. "More or less. But Dalmont has taken him prisoner. I need your help to free him."

Andrew regarded her with openmouthed astonishment. "Victoria, I—"

"Whatever your price, I will meet it."

His head moved in a slow, confused shake. "Why would you want to save him after everything he has done to you?"

Victoria raised her chin a notch. "I love him."

He swore. "Dominic does not love you. I question whether he is capable of such a sentiment."

"I believe he is," she defended. "He has shown me love."

Andrew snorted cynically. "Between the sheets hardly signifies."

Restraining an urge to slap him, Victoria rose from her chair and started for the door of Andrew's dingy room. "Never mind. Clearly, seeking your help was a waste of time."

He grabbed her arm and whirled her about, his face contrite. "Forgive me. Sit."

With an angry sigh, Victoria took her seat again, studying Andrew's blue-gray eyes, red-rimmed and tired, and his hastily donned shirt, wrinkled beyond help.

"Andrew, if it is money you seek, I shall pay you."

A predatory darkness shadowed his eyes. Instinctively, she inched back in her seat. "And what if I want you naked in *my* bed?"

Victoria raised her chin and forced herself to meet his challenging stare. "If that is your price, I will pay it."

His mouth fell open. "Why would you make such a sacrifice for him? He would never make one of that significance for you. Ever. Sacrifice is not in his vocabulary."

"But he has sacrificed," she argued softly. "He dropped to his knees in front of Dalmont, Gaphard, and a dozen others and begged them to spare my life."

His wide-eyed expression displayed shock. "He did that?"

She nodded. "After he refused to say a word in his own defense, yes. He surrendered to protect me, and his sacrifice may cost him his life if I do not find a way to free him soon."

"Perhaps I was wrong—not only about Dominic, but you."

She cocked her head in question. "What do you mean?"

He waved her question away. "It's of no consequence. I wish you both well." He stood, suddenly saying, "Security will be strict."

Victoria bit her lip in confusion. "No more so than Newgate. Are you saying you will help?"

Andrew cast his gaze to the floor beneath him, then let out a long sigh. "I owe him, and you, at least that much."

Through the eerie pre-dawn fog that night, Victoria rode with Andrew. Her stomach twisted with worry as she prayed Corinne could find Lord Gaphard at his home. She anguished that in the precious few hours just passed, Dalmont had already killed Dominic. Even if the fiend hadn't, the government would hang Dominic for murder—unless he escaped.

The quiet surrounding St. James Square made her shiver as she and Andrew approached Dalmont's town house from the rear. As they came closer, silence enveloped her further, the eerie absence of sound reminiscent of a tomb.

They crept through the garden, prepared to meet Dalmont's sentries. The first one sat on one of many artfully scattered benches, trimming his nails with a knife. Victoria watched anxiously as Andrew tiptoed behind the man. The guard paused warily and lifted his head in mute question. An instant later, Andrew struck his skull with a fist-sized rock. The man swayed to the side, his body wilting like a flower in the heat, until his head hit the stone bench with a dull, sickening thud.

"Did you see anyone else?" Andrew whispered, making his way back to her side.

She glanced about, peering through the moonlit night. "Not yet, but I am certain someone will be stationed by the door."

Through the rest of the garden they inched, the scent of flowers, rich earth, and danger permeating her senses. Taking a deep breath, she followed Andrew around the corner of the town house, scooting her body along the shadowed wall, as he did . . . inching slowly toward another guard hulking by the door nursing a cup of strong-smelling ale in his meaty hands.

Andrew leapt in front of the man, clasping his fingers about the sentry's windpipe. Flailing, gasping, grunting, the man surged toward Andrew, only to slump against him.

"My God, have you killed him?" Victoria cried.

"Shhh." Andrew covered her mouth with his hand. "He's simply taking a sleep. Now follow me."

Victoria's gaze left the fallen guard to focus on Andrew as he cracked open the back door and peeked inside. He spread the door wide a moment later and pushed her in. "Hurry."

They entered a dark kitchen still heavy with the smell of yeast and rosemary. Andrew stepped in behind her and eased the portal closed.

"Where do you think Dalmont is keeping him?" Victoria asked.

Andrew shrugged. "Someplace away from the servants, where Lord Gaphard cannot find him until it's too late."

A long, agony-filled roar rent the air. *Dominic!*

Terrible silence followed. Without caution, Victoria raced toward the sound, tearing through empty halls and darkened rooms. Vaguely, she heard Andrew's footsteps behind her, discerned his pleas for her to stop, but ignored them.

Another bloodcurdling outcry sliced through the air. Victoria ran faster toward the horrifying call, praying she wasn't too late.

She yanked open a heavy door before her, finding the steps leading to the wine cellar, judging from the fruity-sharp smell. As she raced down into the cold, musty room, her heart pounded, urging her feet to move faster.

At the bottom she found Dominic and Dalmont locked in mortal combat.

Dominic was bruised and cut, bloody and dirty. His shirt hung about him in tatters. One eye had swelled shut, and his bound wrists throbbed an angry red with rope burns—but nothing alarmed her more than the raw lash wounds open on his back.

She glanced at Dalmont and saw pure blood lust in the other man's eyes. At the sight of the blade gleaming in his fist, coupled with Dominic's empty, bound hands, she screamed.

Dominic's eyes never strayed from Dalmont. "Get out, Victoria! I do not want you hurt."

Phillip laughed chillingly. "Isn't this a loving little scene, the fool and his whore. You were meant for each other. Too bad you will soon be dead, my dear friend."

Andrew caught up to her and paused, gasping for air.

She turned to him, grasping his arms in supplication. "What can we do?"

Before Andrew could answer, Phillip began taunting

Dominic. "You are nothing more than a lowly orphan. Your own wife could hardly stand you."

"Marcella only wanted your title," Dominic returned with deadly calm.

Phillip strode toward Dominic, twisting his blade in the air so it caught the rays of candlelight. "I made her writhe with ecstasy. Only you and the guilt of your words made her want to leave me."

"I said nothing to her. She sought *me* out just before you killed her." Dominic leaned toward Dalmont, defying the knife a foot away.

"Liar! Why else would she threaten to leave me to return to *you* besides the guilt you plied her with?"

"No doubt it was the beatings you gave her. You terrified her, Phillip. I could see it in her eyes."

"Shut up!" Phillip jerked the knife above Dominic's chest.

Victoria gasped, dark bursts of dread paralyzing her. Any moment, she expected to see a ragged gash in his flesh and a flow of life-sustaining crimson.

Dominic twisted his shoulders, straining against the rope binding his wrists. The knife missed his abdomen by a breath.

Dalmont raised his arm again, slashing wildly this time, intent on murder. Galvanized from her shock by his action, Victoria moved to run forward and save Dominic. To her fury, Andrew grabbed her arms and held her back.

Without warning, Dominic kicked Phillip in the stomach. The vicious blow ripped the air from Dalmont's body. Phillip slumped to his knees. Dominic used the opportunity to kick the knife from his nemesis's hands.

Restrained by Andrew's grip, Victoria struggled to break free as she watched Dominic kneel to the weapon behind him and grasp it. He fumbled a moment, then clutched the weapon with his palm.

"Stay here," Andrew commanded as he raced to Dominic's side and cut loose his bonds.

Dominic cast his gaze to her. She felt it all over, hotter than a touch—searing, intent . . . damned. "Get Victoria out of here," he snapped to Andrew and looked away. "I will finish this feud for good." Cold, stark rage etched his profile. He directed a killing glare to Phillip, striking fear in Victoria's heart.

Gripping Dalmont's hair in his hands, Dominic pushed him against the damp stone wall. He whipped the knife up to the other man's throat.

"Now, you son of a bitch," he growled, "tell me how you killed her and how you framed me."

"I would rather go to hell!"

Dominic's eyes narrowed. "You'll be there soon enough."

"Wouldn't you rather hear about how I bedded your whore Victoria?"

Every ounce of anger unleashed within Dominic. Victoria saw that in his expression, knew Phillip's words had pushed him beyond logic. The primal urge to kill branded his dark face.

"Do you think it will bother my conscience to sink this knife into your worthless throat?" Dominic growled.

Sweat began running down Dalmont's suddenly waxen face. "You will return to Newgate if you do."

"I will return there, regardless. If I am to die, you will die too—by my hand."

Victoria watched in horror as Dominic began to press the edge of the deadly blade forward. Blood dotted the gleaming surface, crimson and deadly. The smell of desperation and blood filled her senses until she nearly gagged.

"Dominic, no!" she called.

He paused, his eyes never leaving Dalmont's face. She watched him swallow. "Get out!"

Darting across the room, she touched her trembling fingers to his shoulder. The flesh beneath was tense with his need for revenge.

"Dominic," she repeated, this time more demanding. "Dalmont never touched me. I swear it. Do not let him provoke you to murder because of a lie."

"Is that the truth?" Dominic demanded, his unyielding hazel eyes drilling Dalmont to the wall.

A smirk inched up the thin, satanic lips. "You'll kill me no matter what my answer, so I shall let you wonder in agony."

Again, Dominic inched the blade forward. Phillip emitted a strange half-groan, half-gurgle as more red droplets ran over the steel edge, dotting Dalmont's shirt and Dominic's hands.

Hearing footsteps descend into the wine cellar, Victoria glanced over her shoulder and saw Corinne lead Lord Gaphard into the room. He stood in the doorway, seemingly transfixed by the brutal scene. Panic surged within Victoria, and she prayed she could save Dominic from his own fury.

"Dominic," she cried desperately, "listen to me. I speak the truth! I would tell you if he had hurt me."

"It doesn't matter," he said, eyes still focused on Phillip. "He deserves to die for what he did to Marcella."

"Ah, yes, another whore," Dalmont said. "She craved sex, you know. Did you know she enjoyed being tied to my bed? She liked acquiring bruises while we mated and told me you were too gentle to satisfy her. She deserved every blow of my fist for trying to leave me."

Victoria flinched at the ruthless purpose on Dominic's face as his palm tensed around the handle of the knife, the power flexing his hand. Murderous intent scorched every feature.

Didn't he know what would happen if he killed Dalmont? The government would surely execute him for yet another murder. And this time there would be no doubt. Lord Gaphard was here to witness every last moment.

"Dominic, no. Please stop or they will execute you," Victoria beseeched, praying he would see reason.

"They will execute me anyway." His bitter retort dashed her hopes.

"Grayson, let go!" Lord Gaphard shouted across the room.

"Dalmont is not worth your life," she implored. "You must let go or we have no future."

Dominic's hold on the knife loosened. "What future do you mean? We have none since everyone believes I killed Marcella."

Victoria cast her frantic gaze around for an answer. "Lord Gaphard is here. He will hear the truth." She swallowed against hot, desperate tears. "I love you. We will find a way to be together, but only if you let go."

Dominic trembled as he turned his intent gaze to her. "You love me still?"

Tears of hope filling her eyes, she nodded. "I could not stop."

Dominic's gaze snapped back to Phillip. She watched his hand tighten once again on the knife's handle.

He breathed hard—once, twice—fighting the urge, before he leaned a mere inch from Dalmont's clammy countenance. "I despise you. But not enough to throw away my life."

With that, he dropped the knife. The blade clattered to the gray stone floor, its *clink* a dangerous but empty echo in the cavernous room. The tension left Dominic's body slowly before he turned to her. Gathering her up in his arms, he held her fiercely against his chest as if he'd never let go. "Are you certain you're unharmed?"

"Completely," she said, shuddering as tears of relief misted in her eyes. "I shall stay that way as long as you love me."

"More than anything, Victoria. I do love you."

She held him to her, drinking in the feel of his safeness, feeling the flow of tenderness between them. Tears of gladness fell from her eyes, making paths down her cheeks.

He kissed them away. "Don't cry, love. I am unharmed. We will find a way to be together, I swear."

"Never!" Phillip screamed.

Victoria watched in horror as Dalmont lifted the knife into his grasp. As if in slow motion, Dominic pushed her out of the blade's path, then turned to his enemy. He tried to scramble out of danger's way, but the knife lowered toward his chest.

"Noooo!" She heard someone shout. Suddenly, Andrew lunged toward Dalmont, shielding Dominic's body with his own.

The knife ripped viciously into Andrew's flesh, sinking in close to his heart.

Victoria screamed as she watched Andrew, face ashen, shirt crimson, stagger about the room before falling to his knees at Dalmont's feet, a disbelieving expression on his face.

Dalmont tore the knife from Andrew's chest, then

kicked him aside. Murder on his face, he stalked after Dominic.

"Drop your weapon, Dalmont, or I will shoot," Gaphard said, drawing a gun from his coat pocket.

Wild-eyed, Phillip exclaimed, "But you cannot let a murderer like Grayson live."

"He was never our murderer," said Gaphard.

"Dominic killed no one," Andrew rasped, still sprawled on the floor, his life's blood draining from his body.

Victoria rushed to his side, Dominic next to her. Quickly, she tore strips off her petticoat and pressed them to the ragged, ripped flesh of his wound. She tried to give him an encouraging smile, but the grim look in his eyes let her know he was aware of the blood pooling rapidly around him.

Phillip jumped toward Andrew's limp form. Gaphard rooted him in place with a warning—and the gun's barrel pointed at his chest.

"What do you mean?" Gaphard demanded, sinking to the ground beside Andrew.

"This fool knows nothing," Phillip declared wildly.

"I know everything." Andrew coughed. "Dalmont forced me to frame Dominic for the murder."

Dominic leaned closer. *"What? You?"*

Weakly, he nodded. "I worked for Dalmont. He told me if I didn't clean the blood from his clothes"—he drew in a deep gulp of air—"and take the body to Dominic's lodgings, he would kill me as well. After I"—he coughed—"I did the deed, I left London, hid far away, knowing he would kill me, too."

"He lies!" Phillip screamed.

"Dominic, forgive me," Andrew croaked, sputtering.

"I did not know you. I did not know how much harm it would do you."

Victoria leaned closer to Andrew's prone form. He gasped, then ceased to breathe.

"Dear God," she whispered, rising.

"Indeed, I would say that Mr. Seaton's confession, coupled with my testimony, is enough to convince the judges at Old Bailey that you are innocent, Mr. Grayson. I will let them know Dalmont committed the crime."

"That is not true!" Phillip insisted. "Grayson did it! Do not believe Seaton. He was nothing but a disgruntled servant, fired for poor performance."

"Drop the pretense . . . and the knife, Your Grace."

Dalmont turned crazed eyes on Dominic. "No! He must die!"

Dalmont's throaty scream rent the air, his expression a bloodthirsty snarl. The crimson-stained blade gleamed cold and merciless in the candlelight as Dalmont raised the weapon and charged toward Dominic.

"Stop!" Lord Gaphard warned.

"Die, bastard!" Phillip shouted. "Die!"

In horror, Victoria watched Dalmont surge closer. On instinct, she grabbed hold of Dominic's arm and pulled. Dalmont followed, murderous intent carved into his lined face.

"Stop, Your Grace. Or I will shoot!" Gaphard repeated.

Dalmont charged forward.

The sound of gunfire split the air. Victoria heard a grunt behind her and turned to watch Dalmont crumble to the ground in a heap.

She gasped, mouth agape. Dominic took her cold

face between his hands and forced her gaze to his own. "Stay here."

He walked to where his former friend lay and found Gaphard's bullet had entered one temple and exited the other. Dominic took the knife from Phillip's lifeless hand, then closed his sightless eyes.

Gaphard turned to Dominic. "You are free, Mr. Grayson. I humbly apologize for the inconvenience this investigation has caused."

Dominic shook his head, feeling the world lift from his shoulders. All the hate, blood, and retribution had finally come to an end. "I am free and safe. Nothing else matters now."

Walking back to Victoria's side, he wrapped his arm about her waist and led her outside, away from the bodies, blood, and memories. Dawn's first light appeared across the vast sky in glowing yellows and radiant pinks. The new beginning took root in his heart and soul, inspiring him to seize the second chance he had been given at life.

He turned to Victoria, pulling her into his embrace. "I know I treated you horribly, but I've wanted for so long to tell you that I love you."

Joy burst forth in her heart, only to be shadowed by wary fear. "You believe now that I am not like Marcella, that I would never deceive you with another?"

He swallowed hard, nodding. "You saved my life— twice. That and your honest ways prove you nothing like her. I was wrong to think otherwise. Marry me. Please."

"I will," she answered, smiling, eyes wide with happiness. "No more plans to release me in six months."

"Maybe not even six lifetimes." His voice dropped

an octave as he took her face between his warm hands and whispered against her mouth, "Love me always."

"Always," she murmured an instant before they kissed—with the promise of forever on their lips.

About the Author

Shelley Bradley, a native Californian, has lived in the Dallas area for almost ten years. Shortly after reading her first romance in college, she knew she wanted to write stories that readers everywhere would enjoy. To date, she has won or placed in over a dozen writing contests, including Romance Writers of America's prestigious Golden Heart. Closer to home, Shelley has a wonderfully supportive husband, a rambunctious little girl who is Barney's number one fan, and a spoiled Siamese cat named Merlin.

Visit her Web site at www.shelleybradley.romance-central.com or write her at:

P.O. Box 270126
Flower Mound, TX 75027